Clovis finally pushed Waldo away. While Waldo apologized Clovis held the neckline of her dress and fumbled. When she found what she was looking for she gave a hard pull. A zipper, the length of the entire dress, opened and exposed the real Clovis. That was all there was to it. She shook off her dress and then dived into the back seat.

She did not have to wave to Waldo to join her. Not exactly in a flash, but very soon Waldo was on her, a swimmer negotiating his way, paddling, urging forward, trying to stay on course, then in long strokes, glug-glugging along in the darkness, a swimmer learning the strokes and being cheered by the water itself. It hurt, Waldo decided, but still he paddled toward a tiny flame....

# WALDO

# PAUL THEROUX

IVY BOOKS • NEW YORK

For Craig Wylie and John Lindberg

"... Baader, who calls himself President of the World, is the father of three children. He has twice been locked up by mistake in a lunatic asylum. He is not an especially interesting man, but certainly a very genial one. On the occasion of the death of his wife, he delivered a long oration to the three thousand people at the funeral, contending that death is essentially a Dadaist affair. He was wearing a smile on his lips. He had, none the less, been very fond of his wife ..."

TRISTAN TZARA
*Memoirs of Dadaism*

# PART ONE

# 1

Who would have guessed that Waldo would later hobnob with grown women in hotel rooms for weeks on end, be hailed as a blazing new talent of the semi-surrealist non-fiction novel and be solely responsible for making one of his neighbors a Mother of the Year?

No one in his right mind would associate that man of talent ("full of wit and verve" as one critic described him) with the delinquent boy now standing in the Mess Hall of the Booneville School for Delinquent Boys and watching the cream pie sailing through the air.

Waldo knew it would hurt. It was tilted forward and spun sweet gobs in a spiral as it came at him. The pie hit Waldo in the face with a big blind smash. The pie broke and the juice ran down his neck.

"My mother's got more guts than all your old ladies put together," one boy had said.

Waldo, a bit hesitantly because he was not brave, asked the boy if by any chance that meant his mother was a very fat woman, a big cow maybe?

Then he got hit with the pie. The pie plate bruised his nose and as he licked the cream from his cheeks he sured Waldo. The moon was firm, and soon the moon was Warden Deed. Waldo was being jogged along on a stretcher.

Because the Booneville School for Delinquent Boys was a model prison it looked like a supermarket. It was a sprawling house of glass where boys were brought to their senses and rehabilitated. The day of the whip was gone. It went with the torture chamber and the roach-strewn cells. The guiding motto of Booneville was: Boys Will Be Boys. Where there were once thick iron bars now were lovely large shatter-proof panes of glass, and inside the glass with earnest young faces were once-delinquent boys looking out.

"Through broken homes and bad breaks and bent marriages," said Warden Deed using his own geome-try, "these boys have not been given a square deal. This bum luck starts to harden them up. Booneville shapes them up good and proper, makes them good, grateful citizens and real patriots, teaches them a trade and most of all helps them out."

In a magazine article in the *Saturday Evening Post* entitled, "Warden Deed Wants You—To Listen!" he was quoted as saying, "The only thing Booneville can't offer is a chance to see the world. That's just got to come later."

"At this point in time you've got to remember you're not dealing with crooks. They're not jailbirds," said the Warden, "they're boys."

Waldo was injured. His face hurt from the pie plate and his ribs ached from the kick. He was put into the prison hospital to mend. The doctor came to see him and told him he wanted to help him, that he wanted to straighten him out. This doctor—his name was Was-

bristling hair and a blotched face. Waldo had expected
the boy to be black, but the boy was not black. He was
brown and looked bruised. Waldo had heard a rumor
that the boy had been elected Attorney General of a
southern state; another rumor said that the boy was a
rapist, a cop-killer and a dope fiend; and still another
claimed that he had carried signs and barged into lunch
counters. Waldo happened to know that the Negro's
name was Otto Noon.

"Real gin?" Waldo asked.

"Yeah," said Noon, "we make it out of sugar and
malt and crap."

A guard came over. "Lessee them molds," he said.

They were supposed to be on fudge bars. Otto
Noon produced his pan filled with neat troughs of
fudge dough.

"Cook 'em up and then shoot 'em down to the
wrappers," said the guard. "We gotta get out twenny-
two duz today." The guard turned to Waldo. "You un-
nerstan' what ya supposed to do?"

"I guess so," said Waldo.

"Don't guess," said the guard, "you'll get into trouble that way."

"I'm in trouble now, aren't I?"

"You could do worse," said the guard. "I seen guys
do worse. Noon here'll tell you all about it." He
dunked his finger into the liquid fudge dough, then
licked it. "Help Noon. I'll be over the wrapping table
—so no screwing around." He was gone.

As Otto Noon slid the pan into the oven and set the
thermostat at the correct temperature he said, "This
here is what Booneville is famous for—fudge bars."

"No kidding," said Waldo with not much enthusi-
asm.

Otto Noon walked quietly over to dumb-ass. He spoke softly and as he did a giant of a boy stepped behind him. This boy, oily-skinned and sneaky, was Erratio Lizardi. He was wearing a mushroom-type chef's hat and there was a large banana of flesh on the back of his neck. He placed his hands on his hips, gulped down his smile in one swallow and looked at dumb-ass and said one word.

"Fungoo."

He did not even attempt an Italian accent.

Otto Noon jerked his thumb over his shoulder. Dumb-ass looked at Lizardi and dug his toe into the floor nervously. It was decided that dumb-ass should have the first drink. Lizardi got a glass of gin and gave it to him.

"If he spills a drop I'll ram this here ladle up his bucket." Noon waved the ladle at dumb-ass.

Dumb-ass swallowed the whole glass of gin. Nausea passed through his body like a large descending lump, causing him to bump forward and wag his head. Tears came to his eyes.

"He likes it," said Lizardi.

"Now *you're* in this," said Noon, jabbing the ladle at dumb-ass. "So don't sing or you'll get fuzzed too. And watch out because I been cheesed-off at you for weeks."

"I been cheesed-off at him too," said Lizardi. "That's all I been for weeks."

The boys formed two lines. Noon took charge of one line, Lizardi the other. Both ladled out the gin into the empty fudge molds which the boys brought up. One by one the boys returned to the tables to guzzle their gin. And soon the whole rectangle of glass resembled the model kitchen that it was. The boys stood in all directions; some danced and embraced each other and made no secret of their affection. Some retched.

The boy called dumb-ass was picking things up from the floor and giggling. He said he was tidying the place up. He saw a scrap of paper lying outside the glass, but when he went for it he was thrown back by the clean pane.

Waldo noticed that neither Noon nor Lizardi had drunk too much. They were rummaging through the drawers for things. They carried aerosol cans, cake decorators and frosting brushes to the center of the room. As the drunken boys limped about the room bleary-eyed Noon and Lizardi began dumping chocolate on them and spraying them with whipped cream. The boys, one by one, were turned into giant éclairs. As they fell Noon sprinkled them with chopped nuts.

"Stay loose!" Noon said, now riding Lizardi and walloping the drunks on the head with a saucepan. The drunks fought back with sticky fists. Otto Noon dug his heels into Lizardi and shouted, "Gee-dap!"

It was war. The drunks feebly threw things at Noon and his mount. Noon saw the angry boys, scooped up a hand mixer and used it to bore their frosted flesh. Then the wrestling started, Noon and the others rolling in the flour; meanwhile Lizardi amused himself by writing obscenities in sugary frosting on the boys that had passed out.

Waldo watched a boy take Noon and push him up against the glass wall. He saw figures approaching from the other side of the wall. The guards.

*The guards!* The guards spread out around the glass. Waldo was worried; he wondered whether he should leave through the sliding door. But the guards were over and clubbed him on the head. Blood spurted over the white flour, congealing it into red lumps.

Through this door and over the body of the clubbed boy entered the guards; they milled and thrashed among the struggling flour-covered boys. The shouting of the guards bewildered the boys even more; they stopped leaping and running at the glass. The guards hammered down with their clubs, beating the boys into the invisible corners of the kitchen. Waldo realized that they were expending all their energy to hurt. They were grown men, not very strong, hitting only to hurt. Still Waldo watched.

Soon the kitchen was still, all the boys propped in bent postures, a cloud of flour in the air. The guards wiped the flour from their suits and tried to restore the gray. To Waldo the powder in the air and the gray-suited forms looked like a dream in which he was not involved. He tried to squirm into the back of the stove but in moving he dislodged the front of the oven which fell open with a loud slap. Waldo squatted in the oven, exposed.

The guards turned and looked at Waldo. Waldo trembled and tried to speak, but he found he could not shape the words. He felt as if he were screaming, but he could hear nothing. He thought of leaping from the oven. He started to edge forward when one red-faced guard puffed up to him and pushed his hand in Waldo's face, forcing him back into the oven. The guard was still gasping for breath as he clapped the oven door shut on Waldo.

The sounds stopped. Waldo put his eyeball against the glass and saw the bloodshot eyes of the prison guard not two inches away. Waldo yelled to him, but this time Waldo heard the yell trapped inside his little

"The question," said Warden Deed one month later, "is did you or didn't you take a drink?"

"Yes," said Waldo.

"Go on," said the Warden.

"Yes, I did take a drink."

"Splendid. Now I'm going to be more than fair. I'm going to give you five extra months to sober up. You can think of it as sort of a hangover."

As Waldo added five and nine Warden Deed told him to send the next boy in. There were two boys talking rapidly outside the Warden's office. When Waldo heard the name of Otto Noon he edged closer and listened.

"Bashed on the conk. That's what Pickles said."

"Pickles said that?"

"He'll prolly wig off. That's what happens to guys that get bashed. They wig off."

"He'll wig off," said the smaller boy. "If he got conked like you said."

"Someone said he was cheesed-off at dumb-ass cause dumb-ass called him a lousy spade. But dumb-ass didn't do it. A screw did."

"Too bad."

"Bad? A conked spade!" He faced the smaller boy and said thoughtfully, "A conked spade. That's worse than having the double clap!"

"The double clap! I never heard of no double clap. Is it like the regular clap?"

"Worse."

"You're next," said Waldo.

The riot was soon forgotten and the months went by very fast. Waldo was not sure whether he liked it or not. He was sure he was not making money—he didn't like that. And now he was sure he was in the pen. The ish the books, although when he started he was always interested in them. Part way through each one he became familiar with the characters, the style, the words even. Then they bored sweet hell out of him. It always added up to the same thing: the person with the problem either solved the problem and died, or died before he solved it. The point was in the dying. Dying was everything: the death itself and the fits and what did he say and what did he do just before he slipped off to deposit that rag of a soul in whatever heavenly laundry he might believe in. Of course, between the little sweats of youth and the wobbly shrieks of old age there were side trips and excursions and enough agony and ecstasy to turn the book into a huge bitching bundle of paper.

Waldo became a model prisoner. He started his own prison weekly called *Bars None*, wrote poems about what does it all mean and why is a tree and if the screws are the men in the gray-flannel suits then isn't Booneville the world? There were also his stories: each story started off all right (the boy falls in love, girl runs her hands over her breasts and discovers she is a woman) but they always ended with (1) a scream or (2) dead silence or (3) statements such as "Benny ran as fast as his little legs would carry him to the throbbing little piece called Muriel" or "You mean *you're* the one that fixed the plug that lit the room when I looked up and saw you standing naked..." etc. And there was the poem, "Dirge for a Sensitive Young Man"—

> *A shiny window fell on a boy,*
> *Pain is not something to enjoy;*
> *He tried to get out of the kitchen*
> *And maybe that was a sin,*

# 2

"SEE YOU LATER," WALDO'S FATHER SAID TO THE man in the gray uniform at the gate.

Waldo sat in the right front seat of the car picking at the frayed straw of the seat cover. He looked up in time to see the sign NEW LIFE LANE disappear past the window. Waldo's father ground the gears twice in a row trying to gain momentum on the pitted road.

Waldo's father was talking. He seemed to have been talking for a long time, but Waldo remembered that he had just picked him up at Booneville and that he had been in the car only ten minutes. His father kept talking, and although Waldo's home was not too far from Booneville his father was saying "it's no disgrace" for the third or fourth time.

Waldo's father cut into the left lane and forced a whining blue Pontiac into his wake of exhaust fumes. The cars beeped, honked, and lurched irate in a knot behind Waldo's father who was now straddling two lanes and traveling at ten miles below the speed limit.

"I know," Waldo said, examining a long strand of hemp and wondering why it had been painted with red stripes. "I've paid my debt."

of voice, as if he were suffering physically from a wound which Waldo could not see. "Your mother. She used to cry all the time, Waldo. I mean, *very frequently*—if you get my meaning. But pretty soon she got used to the idea . . ." His voice trailed off.

"What idea?" Waldo said.

". . . and pretty soon she didn't mind when I told people you were away. I always said, 'Waldo's away'— I figured they'd think you were at camp."

"For *fourteen months*?" Waldo asked, looking out the window at a swamp.

"Yes, Waldo, your mother used to cry. Like she did when you poured the molasses into her penny bank. She cried just like that. You remember how she cried when you poured molasses into her bank?"

Waldo tore out a fistful of hemp.

"I mean, why did you have to go and pour molasses into her penny bank? You know she was saving up for Rainy Day Galoshes with fur on the top edge. You didn't have to go and pour molasses into the bank. You know we love you an awful lot—we don't have to *tell* you that, do we, son?"

"No, Dad," Waldo said.

"So why'd you have to pour the molasses into it? You *knew* she was saving up. You know how women are when they're saving up?"

"I don't know, Dad," Waldo said. "I knew she was saving up, though."

"You should know better than that," Waldo's father said. "We've *tried* to teach you the right thing. God knows. They can't blame us," Waldo thought he heard his father mumble to some colored plastic statuary magnetized to the dashboard.

"No one's trying to blame you," Waldo said.

"Lots of them. Millions."

"I might have known," Waldo's father said.

Waldo returned to the car with the cigarettes and the newspaper.

"How much they cost you?" Waldo's father asked.

"Thirty."

"Ain't that Harold a sonofabitch about prices. Thirty for smokes, eight and a half for a new truss. Someday someone should fix Harold's ass on straight. They ought to anyway. Why, that's highway robbery."

Waldo lit a cigarette and blew his mouthful of smoke in the direction of his father.

Waldo's father gasped on the smoke and said, "I know it must have been rough on you, Waldo, being up in that place with all those black Mau-Maus and things. You didn't write much, though. I told your mother they kept you busy with the number plates and stuff like that."

"We didn't make number plates, Dad," Waldo said.

"Well, your Uncle Walter used to make number plates. He made one that said *Walter*, his name you see? When he got out of the clink they arrested him for having *it* on his car instead of the regular one. Walter always did nutty things like that. Made everyone laugh. Walter did. He used to stomp Mau-Maus when he was a kid."

"We didn't make number plates."

"You didn't make number plates, eh? Did you make," Waldo's father snuffled and laughed; it looked as if he would not be able to get the last word out; then he said it, "*cars*?"

Having at last said the word Waldo's father thumped the steering wheel and laughed unashamedly and repeated his little joke as he snuffled ("If you

*them that Ma saves pennies and has one eye that doesn't
look at me so I told them she beats me up every Tuesday
afternoon when she comes home from the racetrack."*

*"You told them that?"*

"Right. That's what I told them."

"What did they say?"

"They made me draw more pictures and tell more
stories. So I did. It was easy, if you ask me."

*"I should break every bone in your body,"* Waldo's
father said, grinding back into first gear and sludging
back into the traffic.

"Say it again," said Waldo.

"You've got a nerve talking to me like that. You
ever notice that? You got a nerve . . ."

"You got a nerve being my father," Waldo said. "Or
anyone else's for that matter. All men got nerves being
their sons' fathers. Kids should have doctors instead of
fathers, if you ask me."

Waldo's father was silent.

"Course, I'm the only son you got," Waldo said.

"Don't you realize," Waldo's father said, assuming
the pain-of-the-unseen-wound tone of voice, "you're
the only son we got. The only one. I'd like to know the
number of times I nearly gave you a damn good licking
and then asked myself, *Ed, he's the only son you got
and you want to lick him*? And then I'd answer myself:
*Ed . . . you're bats*. No, I never licked you once, did I?
I wouldn't do a thing like that. You're my only son—
why should I lick you? You'll get everything I have
someday, every single thing. You'll inherit everything.
Even though you've been away—we all know that—
now you're home with your dad. A kid's best friend,
his dad," Waldo's father said thoughtfully, "although

a nice safe jail, a pen. Waldo wanted to change places with Noon. Let Noon sit in the front seat of his father's car and try to turn away. But Noon was still saying no shit and he had a concussion. "Niggers aren't so bad."

"Aren't so bad? Did you say *niggers aren't so bad*?"

"I know one. He's not so bad."

"Did you say *niggers aren't so bad*?"

"You're goddamned right I said niggers aren't so bad! I'll say it again if you want!" Waldo exploded.

"I wish, son," Waldo's father began quietly, "I really wish your mother could hear you now. She'd die if she could hear you using that kind of language. I know she'd die. *What's wrong with you, Waldo? What is wrong?*"

"Why don't you listen? Maybe if you'd listen once or twice I wouldn't have to holler and you wouldn't have to die listening to that kind of language. It only takes listening to hear, you know. And you want to know what's wrong with blabbing. *That's* what's wrong with blabbing!"

"*Listen? To what?* You want me to listen to you making wise remarks because your poor old mother's optic nerve rotted away when she was five years old?"

"She should have rotted away with it. Then this whole thing wouldn't have happened."

"You want me to listen to you saying smart things because your mother saves pennies in a nice old bank which *you poured molasses into*? I thought you were supposed to be *cured* and come home and all. You want me to *listen* to you? As if putting up with you wasn't enough! Why don't you crawl off with all your Mau-Mau friends."

"Maybe I will."

# 3

I<small>T WAS DARK WHEN</small> W<small>ALDO STARTED HOME</small>. T<small>HE BUS</small>
had stopped running and he had to walk the whole
distance from town. On the way he met a man. The
man walked along with him. Waldo commented on the
sky; it was getting cloudy and gray, he said. The man
said that life was really funny that way and it was no
use to grumble. You had to smile, live, learn and remember that every dog had his day. And then the man
put his arm around Waldo.

Waldo pulled away from the man and ran the rest of
the way home. He spotted his house. It was made out
of wood. It had stone steps now, but there had been
wooden steps when he was sent to Booneville. There
was a new ash can in front, too. Times change. The
house stood still and dead, a dry wooden house on an
empty street. A new ash can. The front of the house,
clapboards and peeling paint, looked like the face of
the man that had put his arm around him. The screen
door hung open as if it was saying, "Life's really funny
that way." A piece of cotton was stuck in a large hole
that had rusted out.

All the lights were out. The family had gone to bed.

he hammered the bottom back and put the penny bank in its usual place.

The bus driver was not happy to take the twenty loose pennies that Waldo spilled into his hand. But he took them when the man in back of Waldo said, "Money's money, I don't see what the fuss is all about."

Waldo rode downtown to Wasserman's office and stood in front. He was about to enter when he remembered that he had not seen his mother; it would not be fair to judge everything at home by the fruitless talk with his father or, for that matter, by the new ash can. He would have to see his mother. He was ashamed to spend the pennies on the bus so again he walked home, threw open the front door and said, "Here I am."

"Howdy do, Waldo!" The voice came from the kitchen.

Something inside Waldo, alerted by the snap of the voice, went dead with a sigh. He heard the clank of pans being dropped into the sink. And there she was.

"What did you say, son?" the woman asked. The woman looked at Waldo, but only with her face and one of her eyes. The other eye—the left one—drifted off and focused lazily on a wax tulip that stuck sharply from a sepia photograph of a uniformed Civil War officer. Or it might have been another war. The woman could never remember, since it was her cousin and not her father or brother.

"You didn't see Grammy when you were out, did you? Say, Waldo, you lost weight! You come right in here and have something to eat. Why, landsakes, you're all skin and bones!"

"You can't take it with you," the woman said quickly, without emphasis. She did not smile.

"No," said Waldo.

"Anyway, it must have let them all in. The dogs, you know. The dogs always chase those funeral things right through the front gate of Oak Grove. Grammy'll be mad as a hen."

"What do dogs have to do with Grammy digging dandelions?" Waldo asked, showing some interest.

"Well," the woman said, pursing her lips into a mocking smile, shaking her head from side to side, and closing one of her eyes, "I know I'd be *pretty careful* about eating dandelions that grew in a place where dogs were. Because dogs," she smiled, "just might have done you-know-what on them. I'm telling you I'd be mighty careful."

"So would I," said Waldo, trying to be unconvincing.

"Your Grammy's careful where she picks her dandelions. And she's very *scientific* about it. I mean she makes a regular study of dandelion picking and digging. Always did, your Grammy."

"Swell," said Waldo.

"But, *dogs*! Why, my land, there must have been hundreds of them following that Czap procession to Oak Grove. Poor old Grammy, she probably spent the whole day smelling dandelions and chasing dogs."

"She doesn't mind dogs. She raised one herself for fifty years," said Waldo glancing up at his mother.

"Oh, we always had a dog. We all had a feeling for dogs—and rats and mice, too. All kinds of animals just flocked to our house. But dogs—they can smile at you." The woman smiled. "Or growl." The woman growled. "I always said I'd rather have a person growl

"I'm just trying to tell you about Booneville, the pen."

"Don't tell *me* what they teach you in jail. I heard all about it from your Uncle Walter and it was no bed of roses either. Don't you dare tell me a thing, Waldo. You forget I'm your mother. Oh, I know how badly you want to get my goat—"

"Who wants *your* goat—"

Waldo's mother leaped into the air and faced Waldo. She hopped over to him and stooped like a gargoyle, "See! you *do* hate me, Waldo! I knew it would come out! I could *kill* you. Don't give me the chance, please don't give me the chance or I *will* kill you!"

"Now, no one's going to kill anyone around here!" The voice rasped through the screen door. "Although someone should get a damn good hiding."

An old woman came through the door and slammed it shut so hard that the wad of cotton flew out of the rusted hole and settled on the porch. The woman was carrying a paper bag, overstuffed, in one clenched fist and a long knife upraised in the other fist. The knife dropped clods of dirt onto the linoleum. She stood eagle-like a moment, her claws full. Then she wheeled and squawked at Waldo's whimpering mother. Waldo's mother was still recovering from the frenzy which had congealed and been deposited into a balled-up handkerchief clutched tightly in her hand. "Let's be reasonable," the woman said, her feet planted firmly on the floor, "so's we can at least carry out our threats instead of letting them hang in the air. And for godsakes, don't get all riled up over *that* mound." She jerked the knifeblade in the direction of Waldo, flinging a cube of dirt at his abdomen.

miss him, don't you think so? I said don't you think—"

"I heard what you said. You also said you didn't like him."

"Doesn't mean a thing. You can hate a person and still miss him. In fact, if he goes off and dies and lets a million dogs in with his casket to pee on the dandelions, then I'd say he's really put one over on you. Wouldn't you say so, Waldo?"

"Eating dandelions? Peed-on or not I wouldn't eat them."

"You better wise up, Waldo. Dandelions kept me afloat during the depression. I owe a lot to dandelions. And you owe a lot to me." Grammy narrowed her eyes and said without moving her lips, "and don't you ever forget it."

"You're just tired, Grammy, that's all. Why don't you . . ."

"*Tired?* Why, it's restful sitting there with those stones. I can hardly wait to be put there under six feet of nice heavy dirt. And when I finally get shoveled into that hole *you're going to miss me*. And so are you, Waldo. Let's get that straight right now."

"Of course, Grammy. We'll miss you to death," the woman said. "You've been so nice to us."

"I *bore* you and six others like you!" Grammy thundered.

"We don't mind," said Emma.

"Emma," said Grammy panting and looking around, "I was an old-fashioned housekeeper once, before you were born, before anyone was born around here. Lived in this house, too, and I was very happy with my chicken fat and my apple pandowdies. I went to church and sang 'Holy, Holy, Holy' and made the best fritters in the church bazaar. I was tough as a

"I won't need these," said Grammy pitching the dandelions into the wastebasket across the room.

"For Godsakes," said Waldo.

"I'm going off to die," said Grammy. "This is a nuthouse."

"They call them funny farms," said Waldo. "That's what this is." A song title occurred to Waldo: "How're You Going To Keep Them Down On The Funny Farm After They've Seen Booneville?"

"My God," said Grammy.

Waldo's mother was still tensed, rigid, her feet apart. She began waving her arms in tight little squares above her head. She screamed breathlessly, "You think you're the only ones that are persecuted. You think Edwin and I have it easy. Well, let me tell you, you're just as wrong as you can be!" She trembled and sweat in Grammy's direction, then in Waldo's. She finally said to the wall, "I don't have it easy. I'm going all the time. Just going and going!"

"I'm going now," sighed Grammy placing her cutlass on the coffee table.

"Nobody has it easy," said Waldo. "But some people have it harder than others."

"What do you know about having it *hard*?" asked Grammy. She put her face close to Waldo's and waited for an answer. Her big-beaked face, close-up, was soft, wrinkled as if it were slowly becoming food, becoming edible. "When I was a girl I had it hard. I worked in a factory."

"They don't have factories any more."

"What do you know about that?" sneered Grammy.

"I know plenty. I can see, you know. That helps."

Waldo's mother began nodding furiously, nuttily. "I know, I *know*. That's meant as a wisecrack to me. I'm

"Look at me when you speak to me," said Waldo's mother.

"I'm looking," said Waldo.

"You're *not* looking!"

"I'm looking as much as I ever wanted to look," said Waldo.

"LOOK ME IN THE EYE!" screamed Waldo's mother.

Waldo went over to the knife on the coffee table. He picked it up and walked to a window box which was resting on the sill and several thicknesses of newspapers. Then he lopped five geraniums and left them hanging from the sides of their pots as if they were nauseated. Waldo kicked over the wastebasket with the dandelions in it and spilled everything in it onto the linoleum. Walking past his mother he said, almost in a whisper, "your eye" and continued into the kitchen, slamming the door behind him. He flicked on the disposal and tried to force the knife into it.

In the living room Waldo's mother stood quiet a moment surveying the room intently with her good eye. With the kind of determination that her mother must have had in the days when she was tough as a whalebone corset she walked over to the window boxes.

As Waldo entered the living room again he saw his mother bent over the right side of the window box pushing the stems of the cut geraniums back into the dirt.

were cured (after) by regular treatment with a drug he could not pronounce, he closed the magazine, dropped it and looked up.

The waiting room was decorated in a jungle motif: pots of ivy, ferns, a vase of hardy mums and a jungle painting which, when Waldo squinted at it, was not of rare trees and flowers, but of millions of people with their arms outstretched like branches and red angry faces like lovely blossoms. There was also a painting with a texture like toothpaste squeezed directly from the tube; perfect for a dentist's office. Waldo reflected on the pictures: the only pictures that ever mattered to him were not in art galleries but in filthy homes and doctors' offices.

But something else added a certain brightness to the room. In the farthest corner sat some colors or, rather, a woman wearing some colors. It was her white knee-length coat, her ochre hat and gloves, her red toreador slacks and her straw shoes with fruit on them that made her look as if she were dangling rather that sitting. The colors pulsed.

The woman was filling an ash tray with bits of a magazine and then blasting the pile of paper with a cigarette lighter which shot a long flame. She cheerfully added more paper and lit it all. Waldo sniffed at the burning paper and the smell of lush plants. He thought of jungle warfare.

When the woman saw him watching her she got up and moved across the room toward him. She was what is known as statuesque, but with a little of the carnival still lingering about her, elegant and fleshy. The kind of elegance that creates silence. Give Nefertiti an ochre hat and you've got it. An orchid sprouted from her left breast. The woman seemed, as it were, rich.

"Too long. He's become sort of an investment. I've poured money into him until I think he's going to break out in blotches—each blotch the size of a half-dollar, like they say. But these things will *actually contain* half-dollars. You know? He probably isn't human enough to break out in a skin disease, though. A bank is more like it. Shrinks are banks. When I was a little girl I had a bank that you put pennies into. Whenever a penny dropped into its stomach a little *thank you* sign appeared for about two seconds in its mouth—it was a gorilla. You'd have to put in another penny to get the sign again. I used to get a big kick out of putting money in it—it became human when money hit it. Wasserman is just the opposite. You put the money in and he turns into a bank that listens to how I tried to freeze a gallon of my husband's martinis with liquid oxygen. Wasserman, like the true bank he is, points out that I hate my husband—a fact that I've known since the day I found some nude pictures in his desk drawer. But Wasserman has certainly been around and he reaches conclusions very quickly. He has a textbook with two pages in it—a very thin textbook of shrink. It has a rule of shrink on each page. One, *it's always people, and never places or things*. Two, *hateful things are done out of sheer hate and never any confusing emotion like love or lighting a cigarette*. It's sensible, but limited."

"It sounds sensible," said Waldo.

"All right, that's my theory after three years of observation. What's yours?"

"I don't know. I haven't known too many doctors—as a matter of fact Wasserman's the first one, unless druggists are doctors, which I doubt."

"Druggists." The woman paused before she pro-

"Like my father's stupid jaw—mostly his mouth.
And especially my mother's eye. And my grandmother's lips have turned to wrinkles. But I don't hate
them all over."

"So they sent you up for doing those crazy things?"

"Yes. Oh, I suppose if it was Hallowe'en or the
Fourth of July I could've gotten out of it. Jokes, I
could've said they were. I did them most in August
and September."

"Those were pretty lousy months for alibis."

"The worst. September was really the worst. I
didn't know it then, but I wasn't thinking about it either. I was on vacation in August so it seemed like a
good time for burning the truss, and for the other
stuff."

"What about September? Were you on vacation
then?" The woman took a cigarette out of a box and
inserted it into a long holder.

"Not really," said Waldo, "I did the stuff in September because I was on vacation still, but I shouldn't
have been. I didn't want to be on vacation in September. You're not *supposed* to be on vacation in September. I never was before—I was always in school."

The cigarette holder hindered the woman's *clucks*
considerably.

"But after I graduated from high school I didn't go
to college because of operations—like my old man's
. . . pelvis, and my old lady's eye. Her optic nerve, they
said. No money, said my old man. So I said to myself if
I'm going to be on vacation I'm going to let him know
I'm on vacation." Waldo paused. "After a while he got
the point. He went to the police station—he could
barely walk." Waldo stopped and smiled as he recalled
the crablike walk of his father, the bones fusing over-

"I like to burn magazines," said the woman.

"I noticed," said Waldo, glancing at the smoldering ash tray.

"I like to say swears, too," said the woman.

"You do?" questioned Waldo, caught a bit off guard.

"Shit," said the woman, simply.

Waldo emitted something between a grunt and a chuckle.

"I know all of them. Some maybe you never heard of."

"Maybe," said Waldo, convinced, as the woman shaped her teeth and lips and pretended to say a word Waldo had never seen a woman show knowledge of.

"You don't look like the type," said Waldo. "That knows swears."

"I know everything," said the woman.

"Yes," replied Waldo sincerely.

"I do," said the woman not in protest. "I'm sensitive—especially to sensitive young men like you. I know you like to give speeches sometimes and pour oil in hoppers—I could tell before you told me so. I know how you feel about vacations. I feel the same way. I know you like to have *fun* and so do I."

Waldo had already said, "I like your eyes," before he realized what the words actually meant.

"Thank you," said the woman. "You have very delicate hands, but your shoes are dirty. I know you have other things on your mind more important."

Waldo looked down and slid his shoes to the edge of the low chair slowly and as inconspicuously as possible. "I'm a slob," he said ingenuously. "I don't have many things on my mind. I guess I just enjoy being a slob."

told you. I've *confided* in you and you're going to do
that to me!" For the first time since they had begun
speaking the woman's face underwent a real change.
Waldo did not like the change. "Don't let me down,"
she added.

"Okay."

"Okay what?" said the woman sitting forward
slightly.

"Okay. I won't let you down."

"You know what that means, don't you?"

"What?" said Waldo.

"The party. You've got to come."

"All right," Waldo said, smiling when he saw the
placid smile of the woman return. He wanted to go to
the party. He might make a little money on it. He liked
this woman, thirty-seven or not, what's the difference?
And she wanted him to come to the party ("Don't let
me down!"). Waldo peeked down her dress. It was just
like in a novel.

"You're a doll," said the woman. "I'll meet you
right here tomorrow at five."

"Okay," said Waldo.

The woman's expression did not change. It was still
bright as she folded her gloves and started to rise. Her
back was almost completely turned when Waldo told
her that he didn't even know her name.

"I don't know yours either," said the woman.

"Waldo."

"Mine's Clovis."

Waldo was about to ask the woman her last name
when the door to the inner office opened. A nurse's
head appeared and said, "The doctor will see you now,
Mrs. Techy."

Waldo had no control over what he did next. He

# 5

GOOD-BYE MA, HELLO MRS. TECHY. WALDO FELT AS if he had just been handed Life in a not-so-plain wrapper: fun on the inside, no return address, adults only. But Waldo was not sure what was in store for him. Mrs. Techy seemed a bit wacky, but she cared for him and spoke directly to him, listening to what he said. Waldo pictured himself introducing Mrs. Techy to his mother: Ma, I'd like you to meet Clovis Techy; Clovis, this is my Ma. And then as he grinned at his mother she would say, You bet your boots we're gonna raise a stink! Mrs. Techy would only smile.

And now it was Waldo's turn to see Wasserman and either get his eyes tested or his head examined. Waldo hoped he wouldn't start on all the God business. He had told Wasserman several times that God wasn't his red wagon or his family's either. They just weren't religious types. Although Grammy said my God all the time, although his father bought glow-in-the-dark religious items, Grammy wasn't praying and his father used the luminous virgins as night lights to the bathroom and to hang things on in the car. They were handy, Waldo's father said.

glands) a change of scenery. A new neighborhood was needed, that was all.

There was nothing bad about the old neighborhoods except that there was no future in them and no money to be made in them. The only pleasant thing was the hatred the old neighborhoods inspired in Waldo; he had learned to hate with edges, with style, almost without effort. There was safety in this and of course safety was the soil in which love could sprout and shoot up, become juicy and then seedy, and finally burst its pod and float out anger, disgust, jealousy, revenge.

But safety wasn't everything and when Waldo thought about it he decided that there wasn't any cash in it. He thought how easy it must have been for Grammy, no great lover of cash, in her factory, working sixteen, eighteen hours a day. Busy as a bee, cheerful as a cricket and steady as a clock, and buzzing, chirping and ticking in the same spot with no desire to move on. For Waldo the problem remained: where to cart that little dry house?

Waldo was brought back to the picture of the bagel and the cruller when Wasserman hung up the phone with a ring and a bang and rolled back in his swivel chair and asked Waldo what was up.

Waldo said not much. He talked about his mother's eye a bit, still blue, about the geraniums, how he tried to ram the knife into the disposal and blah-blah-blah . . .

"What *about* the disposal?"

Waldo reenacted the scene and narrated it. He finished with, ". . . and I stopped the thing cold."

"You stopped the thing *how*?"

"Cold," Waldo said. "That okay?"

Wasserman looked at Waldo closely. Waldo fidgeted.

"Say that again," said Wasserman.

"Well, do I? I mean, *have* to do something?"

"Oh boy," Wasserman whistled. "You got a lot to learn about life. Now life is not too easy. It's tricky. I would even say it's tough. But what you have to do—and I know this because I'm in the business—is *do* something, anything."

"Anything?"

"There are limits. A couple, I guess. Now what you have to realize is when you were most unhappy. When?"

"Was I most unhappy? I've never been really unhappy."

"That's your first lie."

"Okay. I was unhappy when I was at Booneville."

"The whole time?"

"No."

"Specifically when?"

"Specifically when I was in the infirmary."

"Doing what?"

"Getting better."

"Which means?"

"Nothing."

"Right. Go on."

"And I was unhappy at home, I think."

"You think? That's why you burned your father's truss, that's why you poured motor oil into the toilet and molasses into the penny bank? That's why you rammed a steak knife into the garbage disposal? You don't know whether you were unhappy or not? You're a peach."

"All right, so I was unhappy."

said, "Say, Dr. Wasserman, what's a professional man?"

"It's a guy that does something for a profession like a doctor or a dentist or a lawyer."

"What about those people that work on newspapers? The ones that write the news. Are they professional men?"

"Good question," said Wasserman. He thought a moment. "You want to be a newspaper editor—reporter or something?"

"I thought about it. You remember I did a little writing at Booneville, the stories and the paper."

"If you want to be a professional man it's up to you. Just depends on how much you believe in your job, how much faith you have and how much money you make. If you've got faith—not a thing can stop you from being a professional man. Only, one thing. You say it wrong. It's not a professional *man*, it's a *professional* man."

"Sure," said Waldo. "Now what's the name of that college again?"

"Rugg," said Wasserman licking a cigar, still smiling across the desk at Waldo whose mouth was open at about the same angle as Wasserman's, but empty.

Waldo thanked Wasserman and told him he'd do his best. He knew it would be hard, but if Dr. Wasserman was willing to go to the trouble of getting him into college then he could at least give it a try. He certainly had no intention of returning to Booneville. You just didn't return. Waldo thought that all the moving around had proved one thing to him. Even though some things were good you still spent half your life discovering that most things you did were all wrong and that you would never do them again. What of the

# 6

Ignoring his mother's scuffling above, Waldo polished his shoes in the cellar. He lit a cigarette when he was finished and stood before a peeling mirror.

There was not much that could be called professional about the man in the mirror. Mainly, he wasn't a man. It was, alas, still a boy that Waldo saw. And framing his face, beyond his brain, there were hobby horses, decayed ice skates, brittle albums and plain dry dust, residue and so forth that, if it *were* a man he was looking at, he would have burned or destroyed. But he had stored them, all these things which a boyish, if slightly scrambled, ego heaps upon itself.

Well, shit, thought Waldo, what should I expect? And standing among the dusty remains of a past which overlapped on an uncertain present, where walking did not mean moving, where screaming did not imply that someone was giving you a damn good licking, where bruises might be found only on those soft brain-ends, Waldo answered his own question: nothing.

Waldo tunneled through the mess of junk, shoving sleds this way and old clothes and stamp albums that way. And soon he was outside, back at the bus stop,

"You're here. I'm here. Aren't we somebody?"

"Yes," said Waldo.

"Who else do you want? If you want to be greedy I'll let you have your way," laughed Clovis.

Waldo thought a moment. He could think of no one he would want along. He tried to think of someone, anyone, but all he could think of was the man in the bus that wanted to be President. Waldo couldn't remember what the man's face looked like.

"No one, I guess."

"When you come to the fork go left."

They rode on for some distance in caves shaped by the headlights. All around the car the darkness was thickening, and even inside the car it was dark. A small light under the dashboard did no more than make Clovis Techy's shoes look like a shiny clump of fresh fruit. Clovis did not speak. Waldo knew she was there, however, and was even glad that she was the only one who was. Waldo looked across once but could not distinguish Clovis's profile from the outside, now totally black.

"I have the feeling that we're going to get along very well," Clovis said. Waldo said nothing, continued driving.

"They keep this place secret," Clovis offered. "That way everyone makes sure they know about it. Everyone makes sure that they tell their friends about it. That's why they keep the place secret. Because it's good advertising."

"I see," said Waldo.

What Waldo saw finally was a gigantic white tower that looked very much like a peeled banana, pointing into the night sky, riddled now with the wide cones of searchlights. The tower stood erect, oblivious of the

Then he said, "Here comes Rock Hudson." But it was the other Rock Hudson. This man was very short and his face looked like someone had been chewing it and had made a damned good meal out of it, too. He hurried up to a waitress but was out of breath when he finally reached her. He stood before her like a supper of cold leftovers and stank.

When the waitress and the man left the room, Clovis and Waldo took the man's empty table. The table seemed to be in the middle of the general confusion. Clovis said above the noise that she didn't think the man would be back for fifteen or twenty dollars at least. Waldo privately guessed correctly at the meaning of her oblique remark.

The table was behind a rubber fern. Waldo discovered it was rubber, real rubber, only after he smelled it burning. A man a few feet away was wiping his cigar ashes on it absently as he pinched a rather old woman's neck vertebrae with his thumb and forefinger. Apparently, an attempt at eroticism.

The main room of the Mandrake Club was really a funnel decorated in what some interior decorators refer to as suburban Greco-Modern—simulated gold foil, plastic, fur, and Ionic ash trays. The funnel was divided into a series of concentric rings, each labeled with a glowing letter. Clovis and Waldo were in ring N, a respectable one. Ring A had sofas, M had cushions that were either sat upon or thrown. Ring E contained folding chairs and had access only to a fire exit. (The persons sitting in ring E were sullen.) In the center, at the hub of the rings, was a shallow pool surrounded by a narrow, doughnut-shaped dance floor. Couples yanked each other back and forth on the floor. In the

Those six-minute meals, one minute of which was spent zipping the top off the Quikee Banquet ("Cook it in its Own Dish!") and popping it in and out of the oven.

"Asparagus," his father said.

"More?" his mother said.

"No," Grammy said.

"Drink your milk," his mother said.

"Remember how Gramps used to cry?" Grammy asked.

"Any dessert?" his father said.

"You want the world," his mother said.

"Egg in your beer, Edwin. That's what you always want," said Grammy.

"I break my butt for beans," his father said.

"Watch your language," his mother said.

Waldo looked back at the people in the Mandrake. The air was full of smoke and arms and red faces. Some people were merely panting at each other. One man's mouth hung open, as if his next movement would be to take a big bite of his wife, whose back was turned.

But the man did not bite her. Instead, he vomited, his shoulders heaving back and forth. His wife turned to him. She asked him if he had called her. Then she saw what he had done and turned back to her friends. One of the persons she was with said he thought that was the funniest thing she had said all evening. Soon the woman too was laughing.

Other men snapped shut the lids of their heavy chromium-plated cigarette lighters. When they inhaled the smoke their faces registered pain, but the look of pain was replaced by one of relief when they exhaled.

Clovis watched and listened intently. When Waldo

aplomb she half escorted, half dragged the quavering Jasper below. He waved to people as he descended to ring M, near the ducks.

A little man showed some snapshots to the group of people that sat around the man with the newspaper. For laughs, he said, no one gets hurt. The man with the newspaper continued to read and titter. He ignored the man with the snapshots. "And there were signs of sexual assault. With a blunt instrument," he said. The snapshots were passed around. The man kept on reading.

"Clovis?" Waldo saw that Clovis looked at the people with a sweet smile.

A man with a huge badge that said MY NAME IS BUSTER. WHAT'S YOURS? leaned over to another man at the same table and said confidentially, "I'm in wingnuts. You?" But he was interrupting a conversation about death and how one woman really got it in the ear when her late mother died, her own mother, from something or other, no one knew for sure. Buster could not help overhearing, he said, and told about his own mother, bless her soul, who at that very minute not only was completely wormproof but had a bunch of daisies, fresh ones, at her feet. By the time he stopped talking the conversation had turned to breakfasts and the woman who had gotten it all in the ear told about her very special diet. "It's full-bodied," she said, "already chewed and flavored. It has, I don't know, tang."

"Clovis?"

Buster, seeing that the table was a dead loss, tapped a perfect stranger on the shoulder and said, "See that babe with the big jugs? Well, when the Moose met last year in Bayonne . . ."

that's all. It's against the rules of psychoanalysis, he said."

"Psychoanalysis," said Clovis, "it's really giving sex a bad name."

"You think so?" asked Waldo. "I always thought sex had a bad press."

"That too," said Clovis. "But what can we do about it? It's a losing battle."

"I think I can do something about it," said Waldo. "I was thinking about what Wasserman said about college, about how I could find myself there. I said I'd think about it, and I have been thinking about it, about leaving home and finding myself. Maybe be a reporter with one of those hats and know everyone in town, do good, travel around, learn to type on a typewriter and like that. After a while I'll be able to give sex—and a lot of other things—a good name. The only trouble is I don't know much about newspapers and I've never been . . . well . . ."

"You can be frank with me," said Clovis.

"Laid," said Waldo.

"Which college did Wasserman mention?" asked Clovis.

"Rugg," said Waldo.

"I just want you to understand one thing. It's a common misconception among the youth of today that you have to go to college to lose your virginity. That's all wrong. You can lose it just as easily in the back seat of a car, if you can afford the car, or in a movie for the small price of a seat in the balcony. It saves wear and tear. God knows, I lost mine in a choir loft halfway through a hymn."

"I think I need a change of scenery. And I'd like to be a writer or a reporter," Waldo said. He thought of

WALDO                                      73

"So, when do you want to sleep with me?" Clovis Techy asked, getting right down to business.

"You mean *sleep*?"

"I mean *sleep*," said Clovis, getting down to brass tacks.

Waldo shrugged because Clovis would not have understood a twitch. And then he said, "When?"

"When," said Clovis. "You'll notice I didn't say why or where."

"I noticed," said Waldo. But that was all he said for a long moment. Then he got an inspiration. When he saw Clovis put a cigarette in her mouth he thought of a movie he had once seen. Waldo fumbled in his pocket for a match and then, leaning way over and looking past the match to Clovis, he lit her cigarette. That, according to what Waldo figured popular opinion, was as close to lust as you could get in a restaurant. At this point Waldo twitched, but luckily the twitch surfaced as a wink.

Clovis winked back. "I've been reading about colleges," she said. "You might even like it at . . . what was that name again?"

"Rugg."

"Yes, Rugg," said Clovis. "I think you might like it there. Of course, I don't trust these magazine articles one single bit. I'd like to get the real inside story from you."

"I used to be editor of the newspaper at Booneville."

"Sure you did," said Clovis.

"I could report everything to you."

"Sure you could," said Clovis. She looked up and saw the man called Jasper Pistareen starting up the stairs toward them. Clovis called to him.

"The Booneville *pen*? You were in the pen?" Jasper's face crinkled with pleasure.

"Yeah," Waldo said trying to imitate Otto Noon for the moment and forgetting that his only crime was burning his father's truss and pouring motor oil in the hopper and molasses in the penny bank.

"I was in the pen when I was about your age. Pretty raunchy, eh?"

The two convicts shared their joke. "Yeah," said Waldo, "pretty raunchy."

"Sometimes I get to thinking it really wasn't so bad," said Jasper. "I mean, if you can take all the raunch. Lotta crap in the pen. Lotta laughs too."

"A few laughs," said Waldo.

"A *few*! Man, I was laughing the whole time. I was in with a bunch of great guys." Jasper paused and shook his head recalling the bunches of great guys. "Them were the days. I was in with some funny guys —real funny senses of humor, you know. Like this one time . . ." he began. But Clovis interrupted him.

"Look, Jasper, we'll look you up. We got some things to talk about."

Jasper winked. "Sure, you do that. And . . . ah . . . fella. If you ever wanna job you look me up. We'll talk over old times." Then he went up to Waldo, grinned, and punched Waldo in the stomach. "Ya still a kid, too, ya sonofabitch! Hahahahahahaha."

"Hahahaha," Waldo said. His stomach hurt, although the punch was meant good naturedly.

Jasper saw a friend of his across the room. He shouted and then was gone.

"You'll like college," said Clovis.

"I didn't know it was definite."

"You want to go?" Clovis raised her eyebrows to

Waldo thought a moment. "I . . . dunno. I got a charge out of writing the newspaper at Booneville."

"You got a charge out of writing a newspaper at Booneville. If it gives you a charge you should be it. What do you call someone that writes a newspaper? A journalist? A reporter?"

"A reporter. That's what I want to be, a reporter."

"You go to college and learn how. College should be pretty ducky. You be a good boy and go. I hope you won't let me down," said Clovis. "I am placing my trust in you," she said patting Waldo on his left knee.

Waldo felt something come apart when she did it. It was a ripping or tearing sensation, like the crackling sound of a television set being snapped on, a humming as the picture flipped into focus. He liked it. She did it again on his other leg. Waldo was transported.

Just before they left the Mandrake Waldo glanced back. He saw the people sliding around the dance floor and was reminded of those dung-colored lizards that can look like orchids whenever they feel like it. From a distance everything looked peachy. Even the ducks in the pool bobbing up and down among the plastic lotuses. Even they could have been happy.

Clovis had not spoken. Waldo had climbed into the driver's seat and now they were speeding back over the road that led away from the Mandrake. The lights of the club flashed in the rear view mirror and distracted Waldo for a while, and then they were lost.

Clovis's first words were an emotionless request to turn down a side road. The words came out of the darkness next to Waldo. He obeyed. The car jounced on the bumps and then fell into the ruts and humped up the steep grades. When they could go no farther all there was to it. She shook off her dress and then dived into the back seat.

She did not have to wave to Waldo to join her. Not exactly in a flash, but very soon Waldo was on her, a swimmer negotiating his way, paddling, urging forward, trying to stay on course, then in long strokes, glug-glugging along in the darkness, a swimmer learning the strokes and being cheered by the water itself. It hurt, Waldo decided, but still he paddled toward a tiny flame.

nowhere to be seen. He dropped into his beach chair of aluminum tubes and canvas webbing and put his arms on both armrests. In his undershirt and shower clogs he slightly resembled Abraham Lincoln seated wisely and immovably in the Lincoln Memorial. The one people take pictures of. He sat still, his head tilted forward toward the tube. His wife contemplated the book of stamps with her good eye, then picked up the book and slowly pasted the remaining ones onto a new page. The licking noises bothered Waldo's father and he had to turn up the volume of the running man on the television several times before his wife completed her page.

# PART TWO
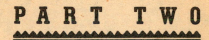

# 8

W ALDO HAD ALREADY DECIDED THAT WHAT HE really wanted to do was meet a nice simple girl, fairly well upholstered and fairly jolly.

His pockets bulged with money. It squirted from between his fingers. Waldo did not bother to count it. Clovis had promised him as much as he wanted. It was a present. If Waldo had counted the money it would have implied a certain price on his head. So he didn't count his money and still it squirted out.

Waldo was thinking of the nice simple girl as he rode to Rugg on the bus. The bus was hot and the dry air was filled with spores and pollen. The bus rocked and Waldo responded sluggishly, his feet on the seat in front, knees against his chest. His head bobbed forward every time the driver tapped the brake. Only slightly did Waldo hear the wheezing of the engine, and once the bus got beyond the numbered streets, the stoplights at each corner, the large buildings, the people running at the cars, wild-eyed, dragging dogs on leashes, the wheezing stopped and the only sound was a steady humming from the sinuses of the engine over which Waldo was curled.

threw his duffel bag over Waldo's head to the luggage rack above and sat heavily next to Waldo. He said immediately, "Can't even goose a broad any more without everyone bitching. A real buncha candy-asses. Wanna cigarette?"

Then the boy went to sleep.

An hour later the bus was still moving. Waldo tried not to sleep. He was afraid the man with the pistol would still be scouting around. Waldo looked at the boy next to him. The boy was still sleeping, his arms folded across his chest. Looking sideways at the boy, Waldo saw the boy's eyes. They were little things, slits, crusted shut. The boy's head jitter-bugged—the road was very bumpy.

"I goosed her," he said, his eyes still closed. "And everyone got mad. Did you get mad?"

"No," said Waldo quickly. And then he thought of the girl. She was a nice simple girl. "But you shouldn't have done that."

The boy's eyes were still closed. "Three A.M. in the morning," he began. "We were near this park watching this lady hitting a guy with her pocketbook. We were just standing there spitting on the sidewalk—a bunch of us, no one knew anyone else, except we were all interested in this crazy broad hitting the guy. About five of us. So the lady was really knocking the shit out of the guy and screaming, look what you've made me do, you sonofabitch, I hate you. Then naturally she got tired of hitting the guy and she dropped the pocketbook and they hugged each other and kissed and she cried. So while this was all going on the guy next to me starts laughing and then he turns to me and says he thinks it's pretty funny, stupid-funny, he says. I agreed. And then he says he knows I'm a Jew because only a

"I know a psychologist. I don't want to be one."

"That's all newspapers print . . ."

"I don't think he's an abnormal psychologist."

". . . case histories."

"So why are you going to Rugg?"

"To see Fred Wolfpits," said the boy. And that was all he said until the bus arrived in Amnion.

Amnion was the last stop on the bus line. It was the home of Rugg College and many laundromats. When the bus stopped the boy with the glasses turned to Waldo and said, "Morris Porter."

Waldo started to get up, but Morris Porter was blocking the aisle and did not move. Morris stared through his big lenses and pointed to the window spotted with dirt. "Look at all those crazy bastards." Then he laughed. He had a laugh that leaped in his skinny neck, hooked itself on his Adam's apple, bobbled that, then unhooked and flew out of his mouth. Each laugh was a separate distinct *ha*.

Morris picked up his duffel bag and walked off the bus. They were the last to leave. Waldo looked for the nice simple girl but she had gone.

"Let's go see what's up," said Morris, and he led the way across the street to a multicolored bar with the sign CHAMELEON painted on a large board over the door.

"Party," said someone to Morris as he entered. The place was full of students. Waldo noticed they had a worrisome sameness about them; their clothes, their glassless eyes, their faces ruddy and noseless. Waldo was surprised at how healthy they looked, stuffed with food and muscle.

"Party," a boy near Morris said, but this time it was not said to Morris. Morris turned to Waldo when they rooming house. I got the whole attic for myself. Fred lives in the cellar."

"Okay," said Waldo.

"Let's go over right now. We can dump our stuff, then I'll show you the other places around here."

As they were leaving a boy came up to Morris and began talking very rapidly and laughing. "Party," was all that Waldo heard. The boy said it several more times.

Soon, Waldo and Morris stood before the large brown house which Morris called the Watershed. On the lawn of the house were little animals—not real ones, but plastic flamingoes and celluloid teddy bears.

Waldo followed Morris up the stairs, left his suitcase in the room, looked out the window at the lawn, then, when he found out the name of Gull Watershed's wife, asked Morris if there was a phone in the building.

"Gull and Dove Watershed," Waldo said into the phone. Clovis said he had all the luck; she would send him some money right off.

Waldo went outside. Morris was on the other side of the street talking to a blond girl. A nice simple girl. It was the girl Morris had goosed on the bus. When Waldo walked over to meet her, she turned and went away.

Morris pointed through the fog that hung like thick anesthetic draperies over the buildings of Rugg College. "Take a good look," he said. He thought a moment, then said, "You know the guy I was talking to at the Chameleon?"

Waldo nodded.

"Well, he was telling me about this party."

"Which party?"

it was at the very top of Campus Hill, dominated, and could be seen from quite a distance.

Waldo squinted through the fog, but he was not looking at anything in particular. "Who was that girl you were talking to, Morris?"

"The girl I was talking to. *Which* girl?"

"The blonde. The one you goosed on the bus."

Morris thought. "Mona?"

"Mona?"

"Mona."

says to me, Duff, he says, you waste a heckofallotta
time, if you know what I mean. And I knew what he
meant. I knew, I'm ashamed to say. And I said to myself back there in Happy, Texas: Duff, when you get
your papers and you're done with Uncle Sam and you
get yourself back to Amnion and the rest, you jest sign
up for a hitch at Rugg College. In other words, wise
up, I said. And darned if I didn't do it and here I am
talking to all you swell guys and gals out there who did
it, too, just like I did it back there in the Second Ice
Age. Hahahahaha. And you all got your reasons.
You're darn tootin' you got your reasons—don't let
anyone tell you any different. You stick to your guns
and you'll be okay. I did. Old Duff knows and old Duff
cares and don't let anyone tell you any different. Thing
is, Rugg can take you to water, but it can't make you
drink unless you're thirsty for knowledge. Gotta have
that thirst. A few things I picked up along the way.
And glad to pass them along, guys and gals. Never
forget, a book in the hand is worth ten in the library.
Education is like a good cigar—you gotta smoke every
bit of it to get the most out of it. Even if it makes you
sick. Especially. Life's funny that way. You gotta learn
to work. All young people do. I'm not talking about
studying really. I mean, get out and dig a hole some
day—get your hands dirty, get all tuckered out, kill
yourself working out in God's fresh air. Buckle right
down and tackle the thing. Take off your clothes—
*coat*, I mean, hahaha, and roll up them sleeves and
jump right in, no fooling. Now I know what each and
every one of you is saying to yourself right now..."

"I said, *good*."
"Sure."

spoken to me or asked advice or said, 'Gee, Mom, you're sure dressed terrific,' or 'Gosh, Mom, this sure is a swell meal.' Other mothers get it. I never got it. I never once remember..."

"Emma?"

"Yes?"

"You like fish, don't you?"

"Yes, I do. I guess I've..."

"And you know that I'm just wild about fresh fish?"

"Fresh fish. Yes, Edwin, I always think of you. I always think of you. I love you, Edwin. Have you forgotten so..."

"No, I'm not complaining again about your bad cooking or your infernal gabbing..."

"No, Edwin, certainly you're not."

"...but do you think that it would be humanly possible..."

"You just have to ask, Edwin. You just have to say the wor..."

"...to buy fish without pins in it. My mouth is a running sore from those goddamned things! Look, I'm *bleeding*."

"Oh, my poor Edwin is all *bleedy*!"

"It hurts like blue blazes."

"Like blue blazes! Well, let me do something."

"Don't get up, Emma. It's too late. Pass me the paper, will you?"

"Too late. I *am* sorry, Edwin. Those horrible pins. Why did they ever put them in there anyway? It's more than I can understand."

"Why did who put what in there?"

"The pins. In the fish. Fish-pins. Why did they put them in there so we could get all bleeding?"

"*God* put them in there. They're *born* with them,

"It's . . . wait a sec . . . the cemetery. It's Oak Grove. Wait a minute . . . um . . . yuh . . . trying to talk to three people at once. Sorry, hahaha. Sure, go right ahead. Like I said, I wouldn't be . . ."

". . . working the daylights out of them, you know what I mean? But all work and no play makes Jack a dull boy. Or Jill, hahaha. Swell, kids, just swell. What I'm trying to drive home is that and nothing more. Just remember Duff Wermy's story about the hill of red ants whenever you get a test. That's what I used to do—and look where it got *me*! Hahaha. But. In closing. Let me thank each and every one of you out there —cause I'm talking to you and you and you—for coming. And remember, don't think of me as your president, although that's exactly what I am and it took a heck of a lot of work and initiative to get me where I am today talking to each and every one of you down there. No, think of me as your buddy, your big brother away from house and home. Sure it's tough to be away from home. You're all leaving houses and girlfriends with heaps of living in them. Your mom and dad worked hard to send you here to get some book learning—they love you like all get-out. Sure, no one likes to leave mom and her familiar old apron and her pies and cakes. I used to see guys—grown men—crying their eyes out down there in Texas, beating their sad old heads on the barracks floor just so's they could get furlough time to see their best girl. You probably never seen grown men crying like babies. I have. And I can tell you it's not a pretty sight. But there's a reason, and a darned good reason it is, for going away from home to make something of yourself. You simply got to work and sacrifice and go away from home. The communists

# 10

THE BELL OF MORRIS'S HEART-SHAPED ALARM CLOCK
rang against Waldo's ear. He shifted in bed and tried to
block out the sounds, but the sounds persisted giggling
against his head. Waldo reached for the clock. It was
gone, yet the sound was louder than ever. Waldo
groaned when he opened his eyes and saw what hov-
ered above him.

His father, frowning, stood over him, his arms outstretched as if he were presenting a gift. In his left
hand the alarm clock vibrated. He held it at arm's
length to Waldo's ear. He seemed to be imitating one
of those useless gadgets that are sometimes found in
gift shops.

Waldo, having just been shaken out of the soft
branches of sleep, was confused by what he saw. In
back of the man with the clock was a woman, attached
to the man somehow, her head tilted slightly to the
side. She looked as if she were about to bob forward to
forecast rain. But the tableau did not shift. The stumpy
man with the clock remained grim. And still the alarm
sounded.

The man steadied her. "Take it easy, Emma. He doesn't know what he's saying."

"Like hell I don't know what I'm saying!" Waldo got out of bed. He was hopping into his pants, unable to think of anything further to say, as he said, "I know what I'm saying . . . I know what I'm saying . . ."

"Why, going off like that. You think a sane person would go off like that? You think a sane person would do what he's done? A sane person wouldn't . . ."

"I'm a sane person! I came here mainly to get away from the whole herd of you, to learn something about reporting. But apparently you think you have the right . . ."

"*Right?*" shouted the woman. "You should talk about right! You're talking to your parents, Waldo. We *gave* you that name . . ." Waldo started to interrupt. It was impossible. The woman was under a full head of steam. One eye seemed to bulge from the pressure. It bulged in Waldo's direction. ". . . and parents have the right to do anything they please! Parents can visit you when they feel like it and parents can turn on the alarm and stick it in your ear if they feel like it . . ."

The man said something obscene.

". . . and parents can tell you that you've done a pretty rotten thing by running out on us like that. Just after you got home . . ."

"Just when you're supposed to be a good citizen and everything . . ."

"What does being a good citizen have to do with it? I'd like to know . . ."

"Well, we wanted to know a lot of things, too! But it took us nearly two days to find out that you were here. And that Doctor Watermain was pretty flip for his own good."

"It's nice of you to ask what we want," the woman said, not sarcastically, but stepping gingerly into the lukewarm bathos that Waldo had expected.

"Yeh," said the man, still nodding.

Nothing more was spoken. Waldo's mother burst into tears. She sobbed. Waldo resolved privately to show no emotion. He smoked.

"Your mother's crying, Waldo."

"I see her," said Waldo.

"You should be crying, too."

"What about? What's this all about? Will you please tell . . ."

"Grammy's dead."

"Grammy's *what*?"

"She never came back!" the woman sobbed. "My own mother! She never came . . ." The sentence was jumbled by more sobs.

"*Now* are you happy?" asked the man.

"Happy? Should I be happy that she's dead?"

"Are you satisfied now?" the woman managed. "Go be a college student now! Say something *wise* now! Ha! You can't, can you?" The woman taunted Waldo with her finger and repeated, "You can't! You can't!"

"Look at him. That fixed him, didn't it?"

"Dead," said Waldo. He shook his head. He sat.

"We're gonna be gone too, Waldo," said the man. "You won't like that, will you?" Then the man turned to the woman and said, "He won't, I know he won't."

Waldo looked up at the man and woman for a little while. Both of them were out of breath. The woman's hands were to her mouth, the man's hung limp near his pockets. Waldo started for the door.

"Where are you going?" asked the man. When the

the Chameleon. One girl, with just a hint of a nose, spoke to Morris.

"So, who's your friend, Morris?"

"Waldo," said Morris pointing, "this is Piper Kraft, Angel Kramer, Wally Dagel, and Dove Watershed."

"So you're Waldo?" said the woman called Dove Watershed. "You owe me a month's rent, in advance."

"Dove's always talking shop," Angel Kramer said to Piper Kraft. "Isn't she a perfect *find*!"

To the amazement of all Waldo extracted a wrinkled lump of money from his pocket. He placed the lump on the table and it fell apart. There were many bills in the pile, and many denominations.

When the persons standing around Waldo saw the amount of money they spoke at once: Angel Kramer said that Waldo could buy and sell Dove Watershed, Piper Kraft insisted on calling it filthy lucre, Wally Dagel said he always wanted to know whose picture was on the hundred, Dove said she would take the rent, Morris gagged, fingered a bill, and said that anyone with that much money was in Fat City.

Waldo gave Dove her money.

"You're new here, aren't you?" asked Wally Dagel.

"Yes," said Waldo.

"Have you seen Marguerite, Morris?" asked Wally again.

"No," said Morris. "Take off."

"Sure," said Wally and he left with Angel, Piper, and Dove who had put the money into her brassiere.

"That's how he makes friends," said Morris. "He asks you an easy question and when you answer it he asks you another and another. As if he's really interested. So you tell him all the answers he's dying to find out and before you know it you got a one-man quiz

"She's upstairs." The girl minced to the stairs, bellowed for Mona, then returned to the now silent group of girls. She suggested they sing "The Party's Over" and was pummeled with the plastic ukelele and the hand. The rest of the girls cheered and clapped.

"Speaking of *par*ties . . ." one girl began, but the girl called Mona was coming down the stairs slowly and Waldo never heard the rest of the sentence.

When Morris introduced Waldo to Mona the little dry house that roosted inside Waldo suddenly had a new occupant; the new occupant was busily sweeping and dusting and freshening up the place.

But there was great confusion in the little dry house. And when Waldo tried to think of something to say all he managed was, "Pleased to meet you. Maybe you remember me. I saw you goosed on the bus a few days ago."

"That's marv," said Mona. "But I'm awful about people's names." She touched Waldo lightly on the sleeve and laughed.

Waldo became a big hand, every inch of him reaching and swelling toward the girl called Mona. He trembled, rocked on his heels and took a long look.

Mona was first of all little, nice, cute—she was so cute, Waldo felt like raping her—and quiet. She stood before Waldo, her bare feet slightly apart. Waldo, the human hand, stared at her helplessly. Her arms were bare, her legs bare, and her neck . . . bare. She was so sweet, so white, so simple and so little that she may as well have been naked.

Mona said she had to go upstairs for a minute, she'd be back in two shakes.

"She can be had. But I never did," Morris said almost sheepishly. Then he laughed. One of the singing the mothers. Grandmotherism is the real problem . . ."

"Why don't you cut it out," Waldo said.

"Why don't you go hug a balloon?" Morris snapped.

"Please," said Mona smiling like a demure referee, "stop fighting. I think you're both right. Now let's change the subject."

There was a long silence until Mona herself offered a change of subject. "You know, my father is really great. We do everything together. He's the gentlest man in the world."

"You're lucky," said Waldo.

"Have your parents visited yet?" Mona asked.

Waldo squirmed. "Sort of. They went back."

"They sound just *won*derful," said Mona.

"Maybe they are," Waldo sighed.

"I'm sure they are," Mona said. "*Mine* are."

"I haven't got any," said Morris. "I used to live with my grandmother. All *she* did was slurp her soup and drive me nuts."

"Where are you from?" Waldo asked. He thought of Grammy slurping her soup and how she would slurp her soup no more.

"A room," Morris said. "When I wanted to talk to someone I used to call up the telephone operator. They got nice voices but I never met one. For a thrill I used to say swears over the phone and talk dirty and then they'd hang up. The TV guys used to come and give me cigarettes and shoot the bull. They were always fixing the TV or the phone or something while my grandmother just slurped her soup. She had to slurp because she had no teeth. She had them pulled. No teeth, no cavities, she said. So she called up a car-she would be able to comment on Morris's story. Mona was tapping on the table with her fingers and staring across the room to the far wall where a boy sang a song. It was about his green love in the yellow mood. Mona tapped her fingers in the wrong rhythm.

"So put *that* in your newspaper," said Morris triumphantly, looking at Waldo.

"Christ," said Waldo. "You really were an orphan."

"You missed the point. What I was trying to say was *I wasn't an orphan*. I had parents. But *they* didn't know it. Those are the best kind of parents. They don't get in your way, they don't tell you to put your rubbers on, they don't tell you not to smoke. I could hang up on them if they did. Now that I think about it, I had a very happy childhood."

Mona turned. "I'm so *glad* for you," she said.

Morris said he had to leave.

Waldo said he had to make a phone call. He found a payphone and called Clovis Techy. Clovis said she was upset. She felt like a zoo. Could Waldo find one? Waldo said he thought there was one nearby.

Mona rapped on the phone booth.

Waldo was forced to make the sound of a kiss over the phone before he could hang up. It took two tries to get it right.

"Let's *go*," said Mona. "I've been waiting for hours."

In the exact center of the Rugg College campus Waldo stood with Mona. It was dark. There was one light burning in Boreal Hall. Probably, Mona explained, a machine that had not been turned off for the night. The mist rose off the surface of the campus pond and the whole night was moist with the fog that

Then Mona screamed. She leaped up and started picking at her skirt.

"Oh *goodness*," she said in disgust.

"I'm sorry," said Waldo hiding his left hand.

"It must have wet right *through*!"

"Wha . . ." Waldo looked down at his spread jacket and saw a large wet grass-stain where Mona had been sitting. Next to it was another large dark moon. Where Waldo had been.

"It's my new one, too. The pleats are *all gone*! That's a crying shame," Mona lamented.

"That's what it is," said Waldo staring at the two large patches of wet on his jacket.

"How's Mona?" Morris asked. "You get much?"

Waldo sat down on his bed.

"You get much?" Morris repeated. He was eating an apple and made loud apple-chewing noises.

Waldo said nothing.

Morris paused to swallow everything in his mouth, then he asked Waldo again, very clearly. Waldo looked at his jacket, then dropped it on the floor.

"I found this when I got back. Someone must have kicked it under my bed," Morris said after a while. He threw a box wrapped in brown paper on Waldo's bed. Obviously Waldo's mother had left it.

Waldo picked up the box. He considered throwing it out the window at the streetlight below, but Morris wouldn't have cared. He recognized the handwriting on the top. WALDO was printed in pencil. He waited, then quickly tore off the paper.

There was a blue shoebox under the paper. Waldo sat with his back to Morris and examined the contents. In the box was a plastic six-inch ruler with a pencil

# 11

THE NEXT DAY WALDO SAT ON THE GRASS WITH
Morris looking at a cloud that looked very much like
an eyeball going slowly through the sky trailing its
optic nerve. Then from a great distance another cloud
followed and that one looked like an eyeball, too. The
second eyeball was catching the first; two big white
eyeballs with a man in each one shouting and pointing.
But the men could do nothing to stop the eyeballs and
they collided, gently, the puffy white eyes crossing,
spilling the occupants, mouths first, onto Waldo.

Waldo leaped up, got his balance, blinked, and then
sat down.

"You're nuts," said Morris.

"Thought I saw something."

"Thought you saw something. Sure. Like Mona?"

"What's wrong with Mona?"

"Nothing. I just said, maybe you saw Mona?"

"She's all right."

"She's been had."

"Who hasn't been had?"

"But she's been had up and down and she still
doesn't know it."

It's usually the first stop when people come to Rugg. First you get your ears chopped and then you get your nose hacked. They call it a nose job. And if you're a girl you can get stuff put into your boobs. I think they put in foam rubber or something. I asked a girl one time how they do it—she had a huge set of knockers. She said, well, you know how they put jelly in jelly doughnuts? I said yeah. She said that's how. But I really didn't know how they put jelly in jelly doughnuts so I still don't know how they do it."

"No wonder all the girls here are pretty! They've all been operated on!"

"They look okay, but the first year it aches like hell. It's one year of earaches, noseaches and boobaches. So they don't generally get had until their second year because it would hurt so much. Imagine climbing all over a broad with stitches and bruises. That your idea of fun?"

"So what happens?"

"Don't ask *me* what happens. I suppose you just take what you get. There are a lot of switch-hitters around. Why stay in left field?"

Waldo thought of those ripe girls he had seen at Rugg. Sweet little things chirping at each other through red lips and constantly waving to someone a hundred yards away. They had little flowers pinned to their big breasts like those rare mountain daisies that only grow at the top of unscalable cliffs where the air is thin. And after a session at the clinic they go to their little rooms alone to ache like hell. The surgeon's knife had replaced the fingers of lovers tracing and prodding the erogenous zones; every delicious inch had been worked over by a surgeon stitching, cutting, stuffing foamy cushions into their bosoms where only unwilling

"You mean, start in? Write?"

"Yah, start in. Write. How else do you expect to do it? Unless they have one of those machines that write for you. Machines that tell stories."

"I'll write," Waldo said.

"Write about broads. Everyone writes about broads. Except make it a little different. Write about dwarfy little broads that turn up here and there, ones that have been had."

"Are you talking about anybody in particular?"

"No," said Morris. "No one in particular."

"But I can't just write about girls."

"Then write about boys," said Morris, irritated, "write about faggots and queens, write about yourself, that's what everyone writes about, don't they? Or write about Fred, there's a book for you. *Fred Wolfpits, Professional Shit*, you can call it."

"I thought you liked him."

"I do. What's wrong with being a professional shit?"

"Nothing, I guess," said Waldo.

"You should meet him."

"You keep saying that."

"Yah. If you want to, you will. You'll never meet anyone in your life like—"

"I collect Orientalia," said Fred Wolfpits. "As well as a good bit of Occidentalia."

Neurotically enough, Fred Wolfpits looked like a Negroid goat. Large flaring nostrils, a kinky beard, and claws at the ends of funky hands drained of color. The beard seemed composed of light filaments; his face was a strange brown-yellow, jaundiced with evil like Erratio Lizardi's. Fred was one of those people, Waldo considered, one of those rare people who did

glad you're studying reporting. I'm something of a reporter myself."

"No kidding," said Waldo.

"No kidding," said Fred pursing his lips. "Here's a
little thing I wrote on that movie actress that passed on
a while ago. I was living in Colfax, California, at the
time. That's where I come from."

"I come from a room," said Morris.

Fred Wolfpits rummaged through a folder full of
press clippings. He had written them all, he said. He
told Waldo to sit down, and he held a leaf of paper in
his strange fingers and began reading: "Dateline Colfax. In death as in life, Bella Feenix—you remember
Bella Feenix—drew a throng of curious fans. New
paragraph. After the mausoleum had been closed and
the mourners had departed, the curiosity seekers—
held back from the star's funeral by the police—
streamed up the road of the quiet cemetery—"

Fred read in a very somber voice. Waldo looked at
him again, at his clothes. No, not a Negroid goat, not a
magician. Fred was an undertaker; now speaking in a
low voice of one of his recent undertakings.

"—they pushed and shoved their way to the vault,
trampling the flowers that lined the steps in front of it.
The women in colorful capri pants and bright sun-
dresses and the men in summery—there's a good
word, summery—sportshirts. One man and woman
wore swim suits. A good touch, no? Anyway," Fred
continued reading, "they ripped the flowers and the
ribbons from the sprays, including the huge heart of
red roses sent by millionaire ex-hubby, Lenny Gold-
quid. The crucifix from Miss Feenix's half-sister, Mrs.
Augie (Hap) Walzer, was knocked down and walked
on. New paragraph, the grabber, you see: a woman,

fin-shaped, was like a great vise composed of nothing but small pieces of junk. Orientalia, Occidentalia.

"—and Sherbert Gaff, inmate of the Booneville School for Delinquent Boys, gave up the ghost," said Fred finishing.

Waldo looked at Fred. "Did you say Booneville?"

"Yes, they lost one a few months back."

"I know," said Waldo. "I was there."

"You were in the *pen*," said Fred, brightening, as Jasper had brightened when he learned that Waldo had been in jail.

"Yes," said Waldo, "in the pen." And then he thought what magic that word had brought to him. Nothing seemed very special about jail, about Booneville, when he was there, he thought. But now what magic it made! It was like saying he had been to college. Waldo thought about this a moment and then he said, "And now he's dead."

"As a duck," Fred said.

"Yes," said Waldo. Waldo felt a wheel in his heart turn and yank on a cord. The cord was attached to his throat, and he felt himself strangling. He coughed. "So you're a reporter. You really get around, don't you?"

"I get around, I get in. If you want to be a reporter you've got to crawl inside people's heads, crawl through the debris. Especially if you're doing the human interest bit."

"That's what I'm really interested in," said Waldo. "I'm interested in human interest."

"Delightful," said Fred Wolfpits.

"Fred," said Morris, "is loaded up to his ass in human interest."

"Morris is so anal," said Fred. "That's because he's impotent."

page, but they don't—oh, I keep busy. I like to keep my fingers in everything, so to speak."

Morris giggled.

"I see," said Waldo.

"So it really doesn't matter what Rugg is like. I don't notice it much and it doesn't notice me—or, I should say, us."

"Me and Fred," said Morris.

"Well, that's nice you collect all these things. But I don't collect anything," said Waldo. "So I get bored easier than you do."

"You don't collect *anything*?" Fred asked, astonished.

"No, all I want is a nice simple little girl and a job on a newspaper—say, that man Jasper's—and a little money."

"What do you want the girl for?"

"What do you mean *what for*? I just want one, that's all."

"And when you get her and put the boots to her, what then?"

"I don't know."

"I'll tell you. Two things can happen," said Fred. "Number one you might find out you're let down. Nothing is so overrated as a good screw and nothing so underrated as a good crap. You'll get mad and beat the nice simple girl to a pulp for thinking otherwise. Or two, you'll meet someone and instead of you picking up that someone, the someone will pick you up and won't let go. And there you'll be, howling your brains out in the air. That's the difference between people and things. People—friends, especially—are bad for the complexion. Give me my knickknacks any day. It's safer."

# 12

"**D**UCK, DOVE!" SQUAWKED GULL WATERSHED.

Then there was a series of loud crashes, the screech of brakes, and the tinny plink-plink of glass dropping onto the street.

Waldo woke up, ran to the window and looked down.

Clovis Techy's white Cadillac was parked diagonally across the lawn of the boardinghouse. The tire marks made disastrous little paths from the street to the lawn. Near the street was a squashed barrel which had squeezed forth wads of trash. And on the lawn a plastic flamingo lay shattered, his body in pink slivers. The whole collection of the Watershed animals had been run over by Clovis. The inflatable ferret lay punctured and flat. The lawn was strewn with counterfeit viscera.

Waldo looked hard. Clovis had not gotten out of the car—she was still behind the wheel and appeared to be laughing, but Waldo was not sure. While Waldo was making up his mind about whether Clovis was laughing or not he glanced back and noticed that for the third morning in a row Morris was not in his bed . . . Waldo

Gull and Dove, seeing the statuesque Clovis bravely freeing her money, said no more. Their arms flew out straight like base-stealers and they skittered about the yard whimpering before they finally decided to lunge for the pieces of green curling in the wind.

Caught in a crossfire of laughter they swayed and swooped for the bills. Gull scratched for them. Dove went nearer, directly to the source of the currency, and gathered busily.

Clovis seemed to be enjoying the scene immensely; she watched the married couple bowing and scraping for the evasive pieces of money, trailing easily from the flaking green torch. It was the kind of scene that is best accompanied by double-takes, cowbells, cymbals, pratfalls and Sousa. But Clovis had now stopped laughing and was getting bored. Her arm dropped to her side and she watched no longer with amusement. She was disgusted. She shook her head and threw the money as hard as she could into the wind. Both Gull and Dove darted for the same bill, cracked their heads and rolled on their backs, feet in the air.

Clovis looked up at the brown house and frowned. Waldo waved, but Clovis did not see him. She started for the front door.

"I'll be right down!" Waldo yelled.

Clovis did not stop. She continued walking up the front steps and disappeared under the roof of the front porch.

Waldo dashed for his pack of cigarettes and dumped out three. He was vainly trying to light a match when he heard Clovis on the stairs. He smelled the familiar perfume and heard the whispering of her straw shoes. Outside he heard Gull and Dove chirping on the grass. There was a rustling of satin and stockings—all the cause most of the original stone had been broken from the foundation to help build the zoo. To make it convincing. There were high walls all around the zoo with tiny windows and ivy, passageways, cloisters, and a subtle Muzak which played only Baroque music. There was a belltower on a central cathedral-like building.

Clovis explained that this building with the imposing belltower and the heavy oak doors was the Monkey House. They entered and saw an indignant mother wrenching the arm of a small boy. The woman was wearing what looked like a gymsuit, blue, with a ruffle of a skirt which stuck out a good four inches. Except for the straw hat with the built-in sunglasses the woman could easily have passed for a gymnast.

The boy cried as the gymnastic mother pulled him away from the cage. In the cage was a baboon standing erect, thumbs around the bars, staring like a condemned prisoner. The little boy pointed toward the inflamed root of the baboon which appeared from a swatch of blue hair at the anthropoid's groin.

Near the back of the Monkey House a rhesus monkey contemplated the act of life with his mate, bored and consumptive-looking, while picking his teeth. Clovis and Waldo did not stay long in the Monkey House, for although it was large and contained many cages, it smelled. The small monastery windows did not admit much air. On top of all this Clovis insisted on sneaking up behind Waldo, tapping him on the shoulders and, when he turned, gluing kisses on him and laughing out loud.

Outside, Clovis walked over to a cage where a beaver first splashed for the viewers, then gnawed green paint from the steel bars of the cage. Waldo pointed to a cage filled with sawdust. In that cage,

"What are you selling?" asked Clovis.

"Ammo," said the man. "Say, you look like a big strong feller. Whyancha try yer luck?"

"With what?" asked Waldo.

"This here's where they dispose of the old ones. Mangy ones and such. Take yer pick. The bigger the critter the more ammo you need. Costs most to bag a lunky horse. You can squash a rabbit for two bits if you're a good shot. See, this way the zoo don't have to do it, and more people come to watch and try their luck. This is a big zoo so there's a lot of mangy animals that got to be chucked away. A good Sunday and we finish the whole mess. Weekends is our best time . . ." The man broke off to sell a whole armload of ammo to a family.

The people were having a wonderful time. One boy was taking careful aim at a cornered buck. The buck finally rushed at the boy and, as he did, the boy shot an arrow into the twisted mouth of the buck. The boy's fiancee mooned and ahhhed when he did this. A few arrows later the buck lay in his own blood and a curtain was rung down as the corpse was carted off. A boar hog with curling tusks and a skin disease was pushed into the cage.

Up and down the cages children were pitching green apples, rocks and arrows at the screeching, dying animals.

"I thought you gave the animals to museums when they got old," Clovis said to the ammo man.

"Used to," said the ammo man. "But the market value ain't so high. God, we get our best prices for the big ones, giraffes, and hippos. Ever try to bag a hippo? You try some fine day and see how far you get. Why, I seen *acres* of ammo thrown at one hippo. Took the

It made Waldo feel good to have figured this out; but it bothered him too, because he hadn't figured out where *he* was supposed to be in all this. He wasn't looking for a roadmap to take him to the right place, but wasn't Clovis sort of a fleshy roadmap that would take him where he wanted to go? Oddly enough, Waldo had the distinct feeling that college wasn't everything it was cracked up to be. Rugg wasn't red hot and this wasn't the place Waldo wanted to spend his life. If he was to spend his life among the knick-knacks they would have to be in a pretty special neighborhood. And if Booneville, Rugg and the Bethesda Tesh Zeitgeist Memorial Zoo weren't the right neighborhoods he still had the pleasant feeling that he was a lot closer than he was before.

"Duck!" said the ammo man bringing Waldo back to the B.T.Z. Memorial Zoo Shooting Gallery once again.

A rock whizzed past his ear and hit the retreating shape of a small furry thing. A woman giggled and a whole family ran to the bars to see what damage had been done. One saw blood. Someone said he was lying. Another rock. "*That's* blood," said someone else. And Waldo walked away.

Clovis had gone on ahead. When Waldo found her she was standing with a whole group of people near a big cage. Waldo pushed toward the front of the cage. Clovis nodded to him when she saw him, but kept looking at the occupants of the big cage.

In the cage were two elephants, one trumpeting after the other. The cage was circular and around and around in a heavy swaying dance they went. Soon the one in front became tired and knelt in the center of the dust. The one in back waved his huge hose of a trunk about college students, how they gallivant around and sow their oats. That's what Waldo heard her telling someone as he paid his money and left the office.

In a jiffy Clovis was ready. Waldo looked over at the bed not dreading what was going to happen, but not looking forward to it. It still hurt a little bit. Waldo almost trumpeted as he slid into bed. Outside in the hall someone (probably the blue-haired lady's son) was squirting bug spray out of an aerosol can; the faucet near the bed dripped while someone in the next room rapped on the wall in time with a piece of music that could only be heard as a beeping drone. The person in the hall paced back and forth rhythmically squirting; rain started and dripped from the eaves, and cars— two hundred in single file—splashed through a puddle outside the window, front wheels, back wheels, front wheels. It all irritated Waldo. He got up and turned on the dripping faucet full. The water gushed into the sink so hard that a fine spray reached the bed.

"There you are," said Clovis.

the Watershed and up to his room where he sat on the
bed until Morris came in.

"Where have *you* been?" Morris asked throwing a
whole stack of books on his bed.

"What about you?"

"I went to classes," said Morris. "I admit I might
blow lunch before the end of the semester, but it's the
only way you can stay at Rugg. Go to classes now and
then . . ."

"I got other things to do."

"You might blow lunch."

"So what? I got friends," Waldo said thinking that
Clovis had friends and that her friends were his
friends. "I don't need anybody."

"Well, you been in other pens before, so you know
all about pens, don't you?"

"That's right. I was in the real pen. I was there for a
long time," Waldo said. For a moment he had trouble
recalling what he had been put in prison for. Then he
remembered and did not bring up the subject again.

There was a long pause. Morris finally said, "Fred's
thinking of having a party. He wants to know if you
want to come."

"Who's he inviting? The rest of his knickknack
friends?"

"So you don't want to come?"

"I'll come."

"Tomorrow night. Fred's."

"I'll be there."

"You don't need anybody, isn't that what you said?"

"Not a soul," said Waldo.

Mona looked up. Waldo stood before her, out of
breath. Mona looked at him blankly, as if maybe she

"He *really* looks as if he's having a good time. Boy, he looks like a lot of fun."

"Who looks like a lot of fun?" Waldo asked quickly, looking up.

"That boy over there. The one that just knocked the other boy over. The one that's talking to the other boy."

"You mean, the one that's pushing the other boy?"

"Yes. The one that's fighting there."

"Him? *He* looks like lots of fun?"

"He looks like *loads* of fun."

"He looks like he's *loaded* to me," said Waldo.

"It's really crowded tonight. It isn't usually this crowded. But it's really crowded tonight. I say *really* a lot, don't I?"

"Let's gooo!"

"Hum?"

"Let's go somewhere."

"Okay," said Mona. "I was just watching these people."

"They're having lots of fun," Waldo said, getting up and leading Mona out of the Chameleon past the people struggling slowly around—puny things saddled with loads of just plain fun.

"They sure are."

Without too much trouble Mona and Waldo sneaked up the back stairs of the Watershed. Waldo's room was seedy. Mona paced around like a rat in a maze. Then she started picking up Waldo's clothes.

"Look," said Mona, "I'm domestic!" She laughed but stopped laughing when she saw that the clothes that she was picking up were the ones that Waldo was quickly taking off. She sat down on the bed glumly, or as glumly as one can look in a darkened room.

reasons? Who could believe all the reasons once he thought of them?

Waldo looked over at Mona. She was still coiled up and still talking.

"... and one time I asked a guy directions. I was on the subway traveling light, no map or anything. He said he knew the exact place I was looking for. He said he'd take me there. So we got off the train and walked outside. He was sort of a guide—that's what he did all day. He waited until people asked him something and then he took them where they wanted to go. The city was big, he said, and most people were too busy to help and give directions. But not him. So we walked a few blocks and pretty soon he said, Well I live right here—we might as well stop in. We stopped in. It was his house, you see. An apartment house. And there we were standing in front of his house. I mean, *it was his own house*. He wasn't lying. He had the key. We went upstairs and when we got into his apartment he made me a drink and then said, what's a little girl like you walking around the streets alone for? I didn't know the answer to that one. I wasn't little and I was going someplace. I told him, I was going someplace, until he took me to his house. So I said, I don't know. Then he went over to the door and locked it and pulled down the shades. I said to myself, well, what's going to happen now? Although I knew. He went around to all the rooms and checked if there were people inside and then came out and said, *where did you say you were going*? I told him. That's right, he said, I remember you telling me. Then he nodded his head and said, Well, there's an easy way to get there and there's a hard way to get there. Now, which do you want? Naturally, I said the easy way, if it wasn't too hard. I had thought he wasn't going to take me there after all. I thought I was going to be a dead duck, all raped and everything. When we got to the place, he said, see, here you are, easy. I took you exactly where you wanted to go. It was true. Then he asked me my name. He said he wanted to take me out on a date. But I said, I don't give my name to strangers, sorry. He laughed—not like a car starting but a nice laugh now. I said, maybe we'll meet on the subway again. Sure thing, he said, sure thing. He smiled. Then he walked away."

Waldo held her hand and wished with all his heart that Mona was rich. Then he slid his hand off Mona's and touched her cheek. Mona looked at him, opened her eyes wide in the dark and said, "Oh."

That was all. It was an *oh* of surprise, but after she felt his full weight her expression seemed to say, "Well, here you are, just like the others" or "Welcome aboard, I hope you enjoy the trip." She looked at Waldo's face. Her gaze stopped there. It did not enter his head.

Waldo found it quite difficult to unbutton Mona's blouse. He scrunched around the bed and saw the reason he was having difficulty: Mona was quickly taking off her clothes, interfering with Waldo's inexpert attempts to help. She took off most of her clothes, but not all of them.

Waldo knocked his elbow against the wall, contorted himself into position and then began disproving every sexual episode he had ever read. At least Clovis knew what she was doing. A lot of things happened just like in novels, Waldo thought, but this (he looked down at Mona) isn't one of them. Nothing was happening on Mona's face. Her eyes were open, staring at

# 14

WALDO ENTERED A LARGE OYSTER AND MET TWO women who said they needed him desperately. We need, need, they chanted; but Waldo brushed them aside and said that he didn't need anyone because he had a lot of friends. The two women became a crowd, reached for him, and threw him to the gooey floor of the oyster. When Waldo tried to breathe he felt his mouth fill with a pasty substance that gagged him like a mouthful of noodles.

When Waldo woke up he found he was sucking on his fingers. He got out of bed, remembered that he was at Rugg College and that classes were beginning (since by his calculations it was Tuesday morning), dressed, took his pencil, his rubber eraser, notebook and half piece of chalk and went outside. The flowers still made him sick. The blossoms on the trees bothered him. Waldo ran down the street as fast as he could, up past Boreal Hall to the classrooms. When he saw a room full of students he went in.

Waldo was relieved to see a map on the wall. A history course, Waldo thought. The map was in full color with tiny names in a long list at the side. The

Then he inserted his little finger in his ear, fished around for wax and said, "This may be a digression, but if I were going to give God a grade on the universe I'd give him a C-minus..."

There were only two more classes that day, journalism and anthropology. The professor of journalism had a felt hat tilted back on his head, his tie pulled down and his feet up on the desk. He was pushing short sentences and gutsy prose. "Give it to the reader below the belt. Make him understand what you're getting at right off. No fancy frills. No kid stuff." He waved his arms. "If there's blood, say so! If someone's dead, where and how! Get acquainted with *alleged* and you can't go wrong..."

When the class was over Waldo took a long look at the professor of journalism; what intrigued Waldo was the hat the man was wearing. It was a journalist's hat, the kind with a deep brown stain on the part that touched the man's head. It was crushed and sweaty and faded and looked authentic. The hat rose and went out of the classroom.

Waldo followed the hat into the corridor where it disappeared among the milling students. Waldo stood on his tiptoes to get a look at the hat. And then he saw another hat enter the Men's Room.

When the classbell rang and the students trickled slowly out of the Men's Room, Waldo entered. His reflection in the tiles made hundreds of rippling Waldos on shiny squares. He spotted the hat, holding a mop.

Waldo walked up to the hat. "Is that yours?"

"Is *what* mine?" answered the hat in a human voice that seemed both old and soft as felt.

"The hat. I want to buy it," said Waldo.

"Twelve," said Waldo, "for the hat."

Sure, John went and told the doctor all about it. But what can doctors do? Doctors couldn't bring his wife (her name was Gladys) back. John hoped that Waldo didn't mind him telling him all about it. Except that she was such a peach of a woman. Always laughing, fooling around, until *bing* she died. Before you could say...

"If you want to keep the hat, just say so. I wouldn't blame you a bit."

It was not such a nice subject to talk about—death, not Gladys—but the doctor told him it would be good to talk about it. It would do John a lot of good to say the words: *she's dead*. Dead. Not a bad word if you say it enough times.

But apparently John had not said the word enough times because John was crying now and saying the word over and over hoping that it would not be the same, hoping it would soon, Waldo assumed, mean nothing. But apparently the word still meant something because John was still crying after several minutes of saying the word, although the doctor said it would be good for John. And the hat, now in John's hand, was dotted with John's tears that had plunked onto it and made tiny black stains.

Waldo pictured the doctor teaching John to say dead. The doctor was saying, "Go ahead, John, it's good for you!"

John said he should talk about it more often, every chance he got. She was dead and gone, dead and gone. Waldo didn't mind hearing the story, did he? After all, she was dead...

"I don't want the hat any more," Waldo said. "You

he had been hearing about since the first day at the Chameleon. Waldo figured he might as well try it. Morris turned out to be gay, the flowers stank; Rugg was a no-fun Booneville and Mona a well-used juke-box that, for a small coin, would play tales of fat and naked cities in which those lost citizens traveling light on subways met for a brief hour of smacky-mouth.

"He's the only great man I know," Mona went on. "Fred. He leaves the room and he's gone for two or three minutes. Then Morris introduces him like on television. And Fred, well Fred stands there and gives speeches on accidentals and dung piles and how civilization is up the creek and we're all lost souls, very Christ-like and well-meaning, and no one cares about anything any more like God and Freud; they're just interested in money, money, money. No one cares about love and goodness and how beautiful it is to see a small naked man feeding pigeons with crusts of bread."

"Fred Wolfpits seems like quite a person," Waldo said. But all Waldo could think about was the two struggling knickknacks on the floor of the coffin-shaped room.

"He's very Christ-like," Mona said, "and he knows all about God without sounding big-mouthed and whuddayacallit. He's terrific, Fred. And when he gives these speeches everybody gets drunk and sings folk-songs about this land is my land and your land. I don't know. It's just the greatest bunch of people I've ever known. They're *real* people. You'll see for yourself."

"I hope so," said Waldo remembering that he must call Clovis and tell her about it. She liked parties.

"You know how it is. People are only looking for one thing."

Fred stared as Waldo brushed past him. Morris, next to Fred, remarked that something was a good joint. He was holding a tiny cigarette.

Waldo walked over to a table and poured himself a drink. The room was filled with bodies and faces; but the bodies did not seem to be attached to the faces. Everyone Waldo had met the previous week at Rugg was there, and there were many more he did not know. Morris was still talking to Fred, Piper Kraft had cornered a foreign student that appeared to be wearing his pajamas. Gull pecked at Dove, Dove cooed into Gull's ear. Wally danced merrily with a hulking girl wearing a lumberjack's shirt, blue jeans and hobnailed boots. Waldo waved slightly at Wally. Wally broke away from the girl and came up to Waldo.

"Hi there," said Wally brightly. Wally was hairy, had bulbous eyes and was very small. He reminded Waldo of a horsefly. "You haven't seen Morris around, have you?"

"I just saw him talking to Fred."

"Is *Fred* here?"

"Fred lives here," said Waldo remembering Wally's angle of approach.

"Of course," said Wally.

"Who's that girl you're with?"

"That's Marge," said Wally drawing his mandibles sideways. "That's Marguerite." Wally leaped into the air and yelled, "Margue*reet*! Hey, Margeee!"

The large girl lumbered over to Wally on her hobnailed boots. She bounced her head once and placed her hands on her hips as a greeting to Waldo.

"Pleased to meet you," said Waldo. He noticed that Margie had a moustache.

"I don't know about you, but I need a fix," said

back of the room. The next thing Waldo heard was a squeaky voice saying, "Getcha han's offa my tool!" Then there was silence.

Nearby, Gull and Dove had stopped talking about Clovis and were now pinching and clawing each other to show how married they were. Dove started telling everyone in a very loud voice what Gull did at night to her, how perfectly Henry Milleresque he could be. Gull shushed her and smiled a bit devilishly, though no one saw him except Waldo.

Piper Kraft applauded Dove. In fact, every time Dove opened her mouth Piper applauded, until finally Dove gave up talking and Piper told every one that she herself adored Gull's ascot—so much better as an affectation than Fred's fuzzy beard, and no trouble to keep clean. She then introduced everyone to her foreign student friend.

Gull asked if it was true that Africans were still anthropophagists.

The African said that sometimes anthropologists lived in the villages, but they mostly wrote books about boughs, bids and brasslets.

At this point someone suggested that Piper Kraft liked foreign students because she collected stamps. The African looked blackly at the speaker and walked away.

A boy in a seersucker suit, seedy with gyzym, mottled with nosebleeds and lipstick-smeared, sidled up to Piper Kraft who was telling the Watersheds that they should definitely work on a *kibbutz* if they went to Israel as planned. It had been a wonderful experience. No. A real joy to see all those people in their natural habitat. The boy in the seersucker suit was grabbed off by Marguerite Bagg-something. Marguerite told the watered. Angel didn't even notice the giantess with the hyphen. Angel held the sleeve of the seersucker suit and watched Wally fastening Fred's cape around his waist. Jane Austen-like waltzing, perverted somewhat, yet still rather formal, she explained to the boy in the seersucker suit. Wally continued to dance with Fred and Morris continued to look for the source of the voice.

Very politely, almost too politely for words, the African student asked Marguerite what was in the punch. Marguerite told the boy that it was fruit punch, gin, and plum juice.

Piper Kraft and Angel Kramer turned sharply and accused Marguerite of being anti-Semitic. Marguerite told both of them to screw. Hearing this exchange, Mona began looking for Waldo, Fred dropped Wally, let him ping-pong through the room looking for a friend; and Fred looked for Morris.

Waldo, drunk, thought of neighborhoods and Grammy. From a certain angle Marguerite reminded Waldo of Grammy, tough, though lacking Grammy's best qualities. Marguerite, he was sure, would never be able to say to her grandchildren that she was steady as a clock, cheerful as a cricket and busy as a bee. He looked at Mona. A nice simple girl was all he wanted, white as an aspirin; Mona looked back at Waldo. She twisted her mouth into the shape of a swear-word as Clovis had once done. But Waldo was disgusted. Clovis was a grown woman. She knew about things like that. Mona made Waldo very sad, just as all the people in the room made Waldo very sad. They were happy and they had nothing to be happy about. What did they know about looking for the right neighborhood? How could they be so sure they belonged there?

as fast as I can: I've had all I can handle. But Waldo could not think for the life of him what the man's name was that offered him the job, the man with the sweaty stories, the one that was in the Mandrake, the jail-bird . . .

The boy in the seersucker suit pushed past Waldo. Waldo watched him cross the room and enter the toilet.

And then it came to Waldo: *Pistareen*, Jasper Pistareen.

Waldo left the room and stood on the front steps of the house mentally numbering all the usable stories he had heard since coming to Rugg. Those stories were worth money to the right person, to a reporter, for example, even if he didn't have a hat. Waldo started down the stairs. It was very dark outside and the insects were making a great racket. Although Waldo could not see the flowers very well he could smell them and the smell was disgusting. Waldo figured the smell was probably greater at night since there were fewer nostrils around to take up the slack.

I'm free, thought Waldo. I'll just find Jasper Pistareen and write the stories. I have all the stories I need: The Sonofabitch Who Wanted to be President, Morris and the Dead Granny, Mona Meets a Travel Agent, John and Gladys, or the Fable of the Felt Hat, The Ammo Man, At Home with Fred Wolfpits, How to Fill a Jelly Doughnut, or the Making of Piper Kraft. Plenty of stories, sweaty and otherwise, and not excluding The Great Booneville Affair, a ballad of sugar and pain. All I have to do is leave and I'm free. Waldo felt like reporting. He looked for Clovis; she had always been there before. Waldo put his coat over his head to keep out the smell of the flowers. He peeped your skull broken? By getting yourself cooked? By paying your fare of two balls for one trip out and one in?

There were only two ways. One was having a friend such as Clovis who would act as roadmap and car for a slightly immodest but not outrageous fee. The other way out was by either dying or by coming so close to death that the pain blocked the doubt that you would ever make it alive. You could either be carried or you could suffer and go. And once you have been carried, suffering is out.

Waldo became frightened again. What if she doesn't come? If she doesn't, I will die—the hard way. The faces were making noises; Fred Wolfpits was tickling Morris and Morris was saying hee-hee-hee; Angel had the seersucker suit all to herself; Wally fondled one discarded hobnailed boot and the girl with the moustache and the hyphen was elsewhere with the African boy who insisted that he was not wearing his pajamas; and Mona, that poor thing, was sitting on the floor and looking like an aspirin that has been dropped into a tall glass of clear liquid—she was coming apart, crumbling softly into tiny sexless flakes.

Little by little the party came toward him and very soon it was only a few feet away. An unidentified arm reached out for Waldo and just missed him. Waldo drew back flat against the wall. More arms reached out and there were shouts this time. It was getting dangerous. In the crowd, above all the heads, Waldo saw the face of Fred Wolfpits. It was yellowish and gulping smoke. It looked at Waldo and grinned a mouthful of rotting teeth at him.

Waldo's body began to ache and his throat hurt. No one had actually touched him but the pain was there,

# PART THREE

# 15

He had been in the same hotel room with Clovis for about three weeks without leaving, even for a minute. And the hotel room was not large. As a result he had spent nearly the whole time "riding shotgun," as they say in the cowboy movies. The only difference was that he was riding shotgun in bed and not on the broken seat of a wagon.

Waldo was getting good at it. Like the cowhand who sits in a broken wagon-seat for a long time he soon accustomed himself to the discomfort, then actually counted on the discomfort. The elbows in the gut and shoulders in the way, the knees in the groin, the wet mooshy feeling, the heat, the damp sheets, like the lumps in the sprung seat were part of the game. Once in a while he would get excited and stab his finger into Clovis's eye. Clovis would moan while Waldo kissed its tears (tears from one eye—that amused Waldo immensely) and nursed it. And Waldo had devised all sorts of ways of prolonging the act. He would—in the middle of it—conjure up the picture of a cow in a field which he had seen at the Bethesda Tesh Zeitgeist Memorial Zoo. The cow sat chewing slowly. And then the ice crust while the snow dropped in big wet flakes on their heads. The child stars, the starlets, the aging actresses lined up freezing in the snow and watching their hairdos go to pieces and listening to the pansies saying that they shouldn't have to shovel the snow, one of them even complaining of an hysterical pregnancy. But this helped Clovis realize that it was all uphill before you could bask in praise from coast to coast. She had what it took and was going places and the sky was the limit, everyone said. Of course, when you're young you just see the bright lights. You never see them fizzing out in the rain and being replaced by an assistant with dirty hands and a tall ladder. That was something Waldo could be thankful for, she said. Here he was on top of everything and whose ass did he have to kiss to get there? He would never know what it was like. Could he honestly say that he had stood in the snow while about nine pansies shoveled and bitched their way through a snow drift? It wasn't the pansies. No. It was the feeling that there you were standing in the snow, a starlet with something on the ball, and where were all those people supposed to be? The ones that clapped like crazy. Behind the trees, maybe? A lot of good the woods does you, Clovis said she thought in the snowstorm, when you have personal appearances to keep and miles to go before a genial host makes you glad to be alive. But Clovis had a that's show-biz attitude toward it all, including the making of her own starlet-dom.

"I've always been lavish in bed," she would say and nudge Waldo's mostly inert form. Waldo would swallow some saliva and nod—not because he didn't know what to say, but because anything he said when he was naked seemed to be off the subject.

said, her share. It was only right, she had given herself, hadn't she?

Waldo, she said, had had his share too. It wasn't every boy that could boast of a mistress like that. He had been places. Probably more than a lot of kids his age. He could thank Clovis for that. Hadn't she showed him a good time? Hadn't she? She wasn't asking Waldo to be grateful, but he had to admit that she had made him what he was. And very soon she would give him a chance to be a reporter. All she wanted in return was her just do.

"My just do," Clovis would say sighing, closing her eyes and placing her hands in back of her head to fully expose in the daylight a naked body that had all the earmarks of being considerably older than thirty-seven. Waldo could tell because for one thing the skin on Clovis's neck was out of whack—it was soft and pouchy and worried looking. "Give me my just do."

And Waldo, sighing and dragging himself sideways into position for the night run all the way to East Cloaca and back for a short snooze, would give her her just do.

So many colors, Waldo thought. Indeed, the wallpaper of the room was multicolored and showed battle scenes and plantation scenes from the Civil War. There were southern ladies and gents with parasols and muskets. Waldo had been looking at the wallpaper for a long time. Now he saw that there were two or three layers of it. Teddy bears from underneath seemed to be carrying muskets, the soldiers appeared to be riding hobbyhorses and even the quality folk from the genteel plantation scenes were being showered with paper hats and streamers. It was all very interesting and Waldo stared at the wallpaper from many positions.

chicken; though Waldo suspected that it was much more than three weeks. He had not been in the room long enough to hate Clovis, but sometimes he lingered in the bathroom expecting to come out and find her gone and her purse on the bed. It never happened. He never really expected that it would. And though Waldo wanted that job as a reporter very badly the thought of leaving the room and Clovis to look for the job never persisted. Yes, it crossed his mind, but that's all it did. After all, Waldo was getting good at making love. He didn't want to cheapen it.

But the color of his skin underwent a change. It went from a vague pink to a faded yellow, washed-out at the edges. Also he was molting. His hair had started to fall out a bit. Everyone's hair probably falls out, he thought, if they watch for it. He took a lot of baths and became fastidious about his nails. He had lost a little weight. He didn't feel badly. He had a lot more than most kids his age. Still he looked in the bathroom mirror a moment before he went to Clovis and each time it became apparent that he had lost his bloom.

But so what? So what if he looked like something from the Zeitgeist Zoo Shooting Gallery that had just dodged a brick? So what if he happened to just find himself in love with a full-grown woman? So what if his hair was starting to fall out? And, by God, so what if he happened to like it? That's a crime? Some people hunt around for years looking for a good place to plop themselves. Here he was mostly satisfied at the age of—he forgot how old he was for a moment but he knew it would come back to him and it didn't matter anyway—and living in relative bliss for a few weeks or so with Clovis in the hotel room. He wasn't asking for much, neither was she. They were happy. Is that a here and zen I weel be happee") or homemade dirty lingo ("I love your slug—put it in my jukebox and we'll have a tune") and so forth. Naturally Clovis was better at it. She had been a starlet.

"You be the blackboard. I'll be the teacher," said Waldo. He threw back the sheets and class was in session. Waldo played tic-tac-toe on Clovis's breasts. He drew faces, wrote swears, and fashioned handles and price tags and arrows all over her jiggling flesh. When he finished he stared at the numbers and arrows trembling with Clovis's laughter. She loved it. She said it was the cutest idea Waldo had ever come up with. When both of them became tired of looking at it Waldo got another tube of lipstick and turned the whole mess into clothes, a tight-fitting sticky red frock with toreador slacks. Clovis drew for a while on Waldo, then they made love pretending they had clothes on.

Afterwards Clovis said that the whole thing reminded her of a story. She had some friends who owned a swimming pool somewhere. They used to invite friends over and then sit at opposite ends of the pool. To kill time between drinks they wrote dirty little messages on their children's backs with lipstick. The children would trot to the other end of the pool where the invited guests would cream the message off and scribble a filthy reply. It was a good idea. They avoided writing about touchy subjects like politics or religion, the children enjoyed getting the sun and being messengers for their parents. A lot of kids never got to really know mom and dad. But these kids had it made.

And Waldo said that story reminded him of the Grammy story. Waldo went on to tell again about Grammy and the dandelions and the time Willy Czap had said paid off in the long run. Waldo couldn't make up lies, he could only extend truth into lies by extenuating the circumstances and changing the names and fabricating a bit. Perhaps, Waldo thought, they weren't even lies, for if he had thought of them they certainly were possible. What could you possibly think of that wasn't possible? Who would have thought that a full-grown woman would take such a shine to him when his mother's left eye continued to give him a cold shoulder? If that was possible could there ever be any such thing as a lie?

With this over and done with Waldo felt a lot better about lying to Clovis—not to mention lying with Clovis—and Clovis willingly paid him for it all. It had come to the point where every time Waldo went to get a drink, every time he said something clever, and every single time he showed the slightest degree of affection for Clovis ("I owe you the world," "I don't think I could ever repay you for all you've done for me") money gushed into his hands. It is a cliché to say that every time he belched he got paid, but several times Waldo belched particularly loud and was rewarded on the spot.

Life went smoothly only occasionally interrupted by the thought that Waldo could make more money working for Jasper Pistareen's newspaper. Waldo became a whizz at making love, too. There were none of those little irritations that are characteristic of lewd old men that want a little fun. He was young. He did not have to get up and make frequent urinations (though, more than likely, he would have been paid for each one); he had no blemishes or pulled muscles to apply cream to; he didn't have a bad knee or any old army or football the scientist's beautiful daughter—the ripply tattered skin of the monster as he dies with a piteous glug and sags to the floor. She was fleshy and uncorseted and she never closed her mouth or even shaped it when she kissed him. She just sponged the kisses all over his withering body. Suddenly it wasn't as terrific as screwing was usually cracked up to be. He had thought that his mind was changed for good. Previously he had been wounded when he threw himself on Clovis, as if he had thrown himself to cook in a big oven. Then he rode shotgun, got good at it and even enjoyed it. Now he sized up Clovis and saw an old dying jelly monster and he looked at himself in the mirror and saw a boy molting into a twig. She looked old, he looked terrible.

Waldo thought that something had to be done before it was too late. He had become a brilliant liar (he told Clovis that he molted every year but that it soon went away) and certainly knew the value of a dollar and had learned to report everything he had seen. There was positively no reason why he couldn't go out and earn a living wage on the basis of what Clovis had taught him.

"I'm ready," he said to Clovis one day.

"Are you really?" she said.

Waldo went into the bathroom that held so many memories for him. He avoided looking into the mirror but brushed his teeth and dabbed his crinkly skin with a towel. Then he went to the closet and got his suit ready. The bug-eyed bellhop brought up a clean shirt and a new pair of shoes. Waldo also borrowed a pencil and some paper from him and very soon he was ready. He looked at Clovis. She was lying on the bed in her usual pose, naked (she looked like a very weatherbeaten saddle that had been tossed there).

# 16

"You got hustle?"

"He's got hustle."

"I suppose I do."

"You need hustle if you wanna be a reporter. And savvy."

"He's got savvy."

"I'm pretty sure I've got savvy."

"No bull," said Jasper. "I need someone with a little savvy."

"He's got a lot."

"Sure you do," said Jasper. "What happened at college?"

"He didn't like it."

"I didn't like it."

"But you were in the pen."

"For a while."

"He did some writing there."

"A little."

"More than I did. It's a good place, the pen, if you can take all the raunch. Anyone ever tell you that?"

"You did."

"Well, it's true. Or it was in my day."

"I told you once this one's a sweetheart. Lady named Czap."

"Did you say *Czap*? A lady named Czap?"

"I think that's what he said."

"Kid had the crud or something. And boy is she up tight!"

"Grammy sort of went to his funeral. She picked dandelions in the cemetery and happened to be there."

"Saleswise it's our best story."

"Grammy died of old age."

"So did the kid! So did the kid! Only the kid was about ten years old! How about that? I told you it's a honey, didn't I? It'll be murder in print."

"That day the dogs peed on Grammy's dandelions. She wouldn't have picked them only they kept her afloat during the depression."

"Did you say the kid died of old age at *ten*?"

"I told you once. A skin disease, I think. The crud. There's a fortune to be made in rare diseases. We're just starting to scratch the surface, too. They sort of grow on you."

"If he knows the lady there won't be any problem."

"A fortune. If he can handle it."

"I was hoping there'd be some writing involved."

"Forget it. If you've got hustle you don't have to worry about writing."

"He's been counting on this. He's been on the edge of his seat waiting to be a reporter—that's all he's talked about for weeks!"

"That right?"

"Well, not the edge of my seat. But I want to be a reporter very much."

"*Very* much. I couldn't get a word in edgewise!"

# 17

"THERE'S ONE THING I WANT TO MAKE CLEAR RIGHT off—my baby, Willy, was perfectly normal the day he was born. He probably caught the thing at school or something. When we found out that he had it, it was too late," said Mrs. Czap re-crossing her legs a third time.

Waldo adjusted the tape recorder. "How do you spell it?"

"Dunno. There's a jerry in it."

"Louder please," Waldo urged.

"I said, *there's a jerry in it*!" Mrs. Czap then put her head very close to the tape recorder and spoke to the machine, trying to reason with it. "I hope you understand that stuff like that is very hard to spell." She got up and went to a stack of newspapers near a telephone. ". . . thought I wrote it here someplace when the doctor . . . *here it is*!" She tore off a corner of one of the newspapers and waved it at Waldo. "I *knew* it was here someplace," she exclaimed smiling triumphantly at the ragged bit of newsprint.

The woman then seated herself across from Waldo once again and placed the paper very carefully on the

the slim bones on the top of her otherwise fat hands. The woman merely unclenched her fist when Waldo did this and let her hand fall limp against the plastic of the tablecloth.

Waldo listened to the hum of the refrigerator for a while and seeing the silent woman said, "It must have been awful."

"Oh, it *was*—I wanna tell you," the woman said. "I mean you know how old men are—real *old* men? If you've ever lived under the same roof with an old man, then I won't have to tell you what a trial Willy was."

"Yes. Into the microphone, please," said Waldo.

". . . not that we minded him bothering and whining about everything. I mean, *Willy had an incurable disease.*"

The woman's forehead wrinkled. She is raising her eyebrows, thought Waldo, although they've all been plucked out. The woman finished with, "I wanna tell you."

"Yes," said Waldo into the microphone, "he had an incurable disease."

"Well, we didn't mind all the trouble and stuff. But he did seem to have," the woman was speaking in her throat, "he *did* seem to have more than the usual . . . ah . . . you know."

"The usual . . ."

"The usual . . . *complaints*, I guess you'd call them; like 'the TV is too loud' or he'd lisp on purpose because he knew I hated lisping. Or he'd fight us—we were careful never to hurt him—we knew he was sick. Sometimes, though, he'd talk about bowel movements all day and never do anything helpful. Well, it was always something, I'm telling you. But poor little tell you the honest truth, I never been in a plane," she continued sullenly, "and at this rate I prolly never will. When I was carrying Willy I cut down to a pack a day. No real drinking. A short beer now and then—I hardly drink anyways, so it doesn't matter, I suppose."

Waldo poised himself for a question, but the woman murmured on, barely moving her lips and still talking hoarsely, down in her throat. "Everyone said I was the picture of health. The *picture of health*. It was a good pregnancy—everyone said so. My sister-in-law came in on Fridays to get the house picked up. I quit my job at the electronics plant . . ."

Waldo fiddled with the knobs of the tape recorder and tried to think of a good question to ask Mrs. Czap. But he could think of nothing.

". . . so the doctor was real happy with my progress. I was feeling fine and I didn't have any whuddayacallits . . . ah . . . discharges, at all. Like I say, everyone said I was the picture of health."

Both were silent for a while. Mrs. Czap looked around the room rather furtively, as if looking for her lost momentum. Waldo began to speak, but he was interrupted by the woman, and when they were both speaking at once Waldo saw that she had no intention of stopping. Waldo clicked his retractable pen in protest and let the woman continue into the microphone.

"And after a year," she was saying, "he showed signs of being a pretty good-looking kid. No Ronald Fairbanks or anything like that, you understand, but . . . not a *bad-looking kid*. Had his old man's—" The woman mumbled a prayer. ". . . eyes and nose. My mouth. That's all he had of ours, though."

"Do you have any pictures of him?"

"Of who?"

done it all if it wasn't for Willy. We figured we owed it to the poor little kid."

"He was your son."

"You'll never know the heartbreak of it all."

"I remember Grammy telling me," said Waldo.

"But that wasn't all of it. Not by a long shot. We got a regular little casket for him and even tiny little flowers and like that. What I mean is, everything was the same except smaller. As small as we could get it, really." Waldo looked up and when his eyes met those of the woman he looked down again. "What I mean is we gave the little guy a regular little funeral with candles and all. And people sent stuff . . ."

"Everyone knew Willy," said Waldo trying to think if he had ever seen him around the neighborhood.

"*I'll say* they all knew Willy," the woman said. "Why, I'm telling you when it came to cookies and milk he *cleaned* up. They all adored him. I mean," she nodded, "*adored* him."

"So, naturally they all came to the funeral."

"Sure, why not? They figured it'd only be an hour or so. It was for Willy, they figured."

"Of course. And for you too, Mrs. Czap."

"Oh, they prolly figured it would help us out of a spot."

"A spot?"

"Well, I'm not saying that Willy was *unpopular*—I told you about the cookies and milk—but, after all, there was only this street. That's not many people when you think about it. So, there wasn't enough for a real funeral unless almost everybody came."

"No," said Waldo.

"No," said the woman.

"Must have been terrible."

though it had a ramp and was real nice plastic and cost fifty cents. I don't know. Maybe he picked him up too much, you know, *handled* him ... or maybe not enough ..." Her voice trailed off as if her mind were narrowing the way her eyes were. She said, "I don't know" again.

"Willy was attached to that turtle. Do you have a picture of the tur ..."

"... anyway, he got soft. His shell. Although it wasn't colored like most two-bit turtles ... and he died."

"... maybe Willy posing with the turtle ..."

"We wanted to buy him another one. It's only a quarter turtle, I said to him. But he only wanted that old soft turtle with the green shell. Green shells are hard to get—mostly they have colors or flowers on them. And Willy's turtle was squishy and smelled and I couldn't look at it after he dug it up—it got pieces of lint on it from being carried around in his pocket. Pretty soon it wasn't a turtle at all but a linty old ball of dead." The woman's voice droned into the machine. It sounded as if she were speaking through a network of rubber bands.

"So I guess I'll check the school for pictures," Waldo said.

"I used to hear him cry sometimes at night, Willy."

There was silence in the room for a long time. Even the woman's last word, the name, was gone. The sun going down illuminated the tops of things: the broken lamp on the table, the head of the woman, Mrs. Czap, her hair in wild Gorgon strands stuck out, made gold by the late afternoon sun. The plaster Christ pocked under the beams and the bread was lost in the shadow of the bank.

me to tell him that I made him like that, which wasn't true because I told you myself I loved him and I did. I couldn't come right out and say, *I didn't do it to you, Willy* because he never said anything—just looked at me with his old body and his little hands with long fingernails around the bars of the playpen..."

"That disease," Waldo said. "Horrible."

"It was him. And it got so... I couldn't even..." The woman gasped once. Then she said, "look." She sobbed dryly, still gasping, then shut her mouth tight and left Waldo and the microphone and looked at the sun for a long while.

"My feet swelled up," Mrs. Czap said at last. "And so did my legs. Pretty soon I knew it was going to come any day." She paused. "The night I had the baby..." She stopped, then picked up again. "The night I had the baby Willy didn't sleep in the playpen like usual. He went for a walk—even though we told him never go out of the house. He walked all the way outside of town where the big trees are... the ones on the calendars."

Waldo could not think of the name of the big trees.

"And that's where they found him next morning. All curled up and lying at the foot of the big trees. They took a picture of him lying there with a blanket over him..."

"It must have been a very rare disease," Waldo said just remembering that a reporter has to have a lot of hustle and a lot of savvy.

"...and I was in the hospital with the baby three more days and on the fourth *it* died from something. I was still getting sick every morning. But pretty soon I stopped. Like before."

Waldo saw that the woman had stopped for good.

"We'll go piggyback," said Mrs. Czap. "You always liked piggyback rides."

She doesn't want the money. The death of Willy has affected her good sense. She's crazy. "I'll give you a tip if you let me go," said Waldo. "A fin if you stop squeezing me like that."

Money was no object. Mrs. Czap held on and Waldo couldn't budge her. He had made up his mind that he would do nothing. What right had this woman to make advances? He ignored Mrs. Czap's rude suggestions and cheap tricks and tore himself away.

"Please!" said Mrs. Czap smoothing her dress. "Willy!"

"You're going to make a bundle on this story," said Waldo. "You want the world?"

A fine thing, Waldo thought. I shouldn't have led her on. Shouldn't have teased her. But what right does a woman her age have to try that hanky-panky with me?

Waldo picked up his tape recorder and, feeling very noble and clean, went directly to Jasper's office. *Dying Mother Tells All* appeared in the morning edition.

the other side and saw the blue one looking at him. It gave him the creeps. He went to the other side of the room and sat down.

Waldo's mother marched across the room and tripped over Waldo's stretched-out legs.

"Will you watch what you're doing!" she screamed.

"Ma?" Waldo said softly.

"What do you want?" Waldo was right. She *did* have the uglies. Waldo felt like leaving.

"I'm back."

"I see you."

"You do?"

"I asked you once, what do you want?" Waldo's mother trembled, all the gruesome little complaints curdled in her voice as she spoke.

"Do I have to want something to come home?"

"Other people don't. You do. Now tell me and make it snappy. I haven't got time to talk. You can see how busy I am. What's that stuff on your skin and for goodness sake what happened to your hair?"

"Nothing."

"Nothing? Look at your hair, Waldo. Look at your hair and tell me that's nothing."

"I've seen it. It's nothing."

"Is it one of those fancy haircuts?"

"No."

"Is it some kind of disease?"

"No."

"Well, I don't like the looks of that hair one bit. If you think you're going to waltz in this house with hair like that you've got another think coming. I won't allow it."

"I can't help it. It just got that way."

"Don't come in here and tell me you can't help it.

you've been plastering it with goo. It's hateful hair and I won't look at it a minute longer. Go away, Waldo, I don't want to look at your hair."

"Don't look, then. You don't *have* to look. I just came home to see how you and Dad are. I've been busy or I would've come sooner."

"It looks doggy, that hair. It looks crumby."

"Will you stop talking about my hair!" Waldo got to his feet and faced his mother. His mother's right eye was staring at his hair.

"It breaks my heart to look at your hair," Waldo's mother said.

"No one's asking you to look. Now will you tell me how you and Dad are? Is everything okay?"

"How could you come home looking like that? Are you a beatnik? Is that why your hair looks so funny?"

"It's a very rare disease."

"Well, you may think it's all right to look that way. You don't have to answer to the neighbors. You just come and go like this was a hotel. Is that the *style* nowadays? Is it the style to insult your mother and make your hair awful because you know how much it bothers your mother to have it that way? I wish your father were here—he'd tell you, Waldo, you look queer as an ash barrel!"

"I bought him a new truss," said Waldo, fidgeting with a large box and pulling out something that looked like a rucksack from a nest of tissue paper.

"We don't want your filthy presents. Why don't you just take it back where you got it? Why don't you go!"

Waldo started to back up. He said nothing for a moment or two and then he said, very quietly, "Look, if I do—if I *do* go away—I'll never set foot in this house again, I'll never listen to one more word from with that she picked up a cushion, went behind the sofa and lay down, out of sight.

"What are you doing?"

The voice was muffled. It said: "I can't talk to you if I have to look at your disgusting hair. Please sit down, Waldo. If you want to talk we can talk—it'll be like talking on the phone. Fun. You never called up once and told us anything . . ." The voice stopped.

Waldo looked at his mother—or at as much of his mother as he could see. There was the sofa, battered, with the springs protruding from the cushions and other slighter stony bulges. It too looked like Clovis's jelly-monster, fleshy, bulgy. But it was so big that soon Waldo imagined that it was an old headless animal with short legs. And this fat frayed beast was squatting on his mother whose feet protruded and showed her to be cold and dumb. Indeed, those gnarled silent feet were all that remained of his mother. Waldo sat down in a chair opposite the squatting sofa. He lit a cigarette and waited for a voice.

He heard the hucking of phlegm and then, "Waldo, is that *you*?" His mother actually spoke as if she were talking on the telephone.

"Yes."

"You okay?"

"Yes."

"No ills?"

"No."

"Good."

"You?"

"We're all fine here. Tip-top."

"Good."

There was a pause, a buzz in Waldo's ears.

"Waldo?"

". . . her name is a household word! That little beast used to come over here begging for a glass of milk. And I was stupid enough to give it to him. It's probably *my* fault he lived so long!"

Waldo's mother's feet drummed up and down as if she was trapped under the sofa and struggling to get free. Each time she spoke she thumped her feet on the floor, she cursed and apparently was banging her head as well because each foot-thump was accompanied by another thump, muffled, from the hidden end of his mother. She went on and on, enumerating Sybil Czap's many prizes and great good luck in having an ordinary son with a rare disease. Sybil had had her hair done, her face lifted, and had been deluged with money and marriage proposals—men from all over the world sought the hand that patted the prematurely grizzled head of Willy.

"You've ruined us, Waldo!" She screamed. "We're ruined for *life* and it's all your doing. They've turned her house into a museum and set up booths outside selling Willy Czap sweatshirts. Why, everything that little boy *touched* is worth a mint!"

"So she got a little dough. So what? You haven't given me any good reasons why you should go off your head about this . . ."

"*Reasons!* Don't talk to me about reasons, Waldo. I'm your mother—have you forgotten that? Reasons! Why your father works and slaves like a dog to keep us in good healthy food. I do my best. And *you*—you turn around and slap us in the face. That's the last straw! I don't have to take any more from you. I don't have to if I don't want to. Who ever said kids are grateful? I'd like to know. I'd kill him with my bare hands! Grateful? My eye! You spit at us and then run

"So you *think* about her! That's big of you, mighty big! But what do you go and do? You go and write about Sybil Czap and don't give a hoot about your family. No. You never did and you never will because it's too late now. These things are only good once. If you were to write about a dead lady now they'd all think we were after the money."

"Which money?"

"Sure you think about Grammy, sure you do. The next thing you'll tell me is that you loved her very much."

"I did—I'm pretty sure I did."

"That's a lie."

"It's not a lie. I loved her."

"It's a lie. You weren't even listening when we told you she was dead and would never come back. You couldn't have been or you wouldn't have done what you did. You would have taken some pity on her, on us, maybe. Maybe on us who love you! Instead you go and take a perfect stranger, Sybil Czap, who never gave you a second look. I'm not complaining, Waldo. I'm just saying that you can't go around telling people that I'm your mother and that you loved Grammy when you didn't have the common decency to write your story about Grammy's death."

"I never thought of it, come to think of it."

"Because you're rotten to the core, that's why."

Waldo wasn't really sure whether he hadn't written about Grammy because he loved her or because there was no money in it. Lots of other people had written about the dear dead days passed in their Grammy's stuffy, gingerbread-smelling parlors. The lovable shrunken Grammys. If he had loved her, he thought, what good would it do to talk about it? It's the stuff greedy face staring over the top of the sofa—that was his mother, she was entitled to it free of charge. Waldo was frightened. He knew what was coming. She would start that why-did-you-do-it-to-us business all over again and then expect Waldo to climb all over her. No, he was a one-woman man and he could not betray Clovis.

"I'm sick of it," said Waldo's mother. "I can't do it any longer. I don't want to be your mother any more —there are too many heartaches and setbacks. I just look at your hair and I get sick, and then I think of what you did to us and how you forgot Grammy that way and I want to kill you. I can't go on like this— you're no use to us any more. I'm through."

Good, thought Waldo, she doesn't want to be my mother. That means she's not entitled to anything free. Yes, she looks very hungry, but that doesn't give her any rights.

Waldo got up. His mother stared at his hair and almost smiled, as if someday she would get her chance to tell about how he had died. After a decent period of time elapsed, after people forgot about Sybil Czap and Willy, Waldo's mother would tell about him and get rich. So that's how it is, Waldo thought. He went directly outside and scrambled into Clovis's Cadillac and took off like a shot. It was late and Clovis had not had her just do. There was no need ever to come back home again.

containing unforgettable moments in the Menagerie we call Life Itself. Waldo was well on his way to becoming nothing less than the most gifted writer of ripe mid-century Americana. His reportage was flawless, his genius keen and sure and fine, and he had succeeded in getting down on paper and ordering between covers the only non-fiction surrealistic story ever written.

Whenever she read these reviews in the papers Clovis said the same thing: "It's enough to give you a shit-fit!" She felt threatened by the praise and made Waldo promise that he would never leave her, not for a minute. She had made him what he was, she said, and he couldn't bite the hand that was feeding him just because it was the closest one to his mouth.

So they were four: Waldo, Clovis, Jasper and Mrs. Czap. Jasper bought a bus and they planned a tour together. This arrangement pleased Mrs. Czap who was still convinced that Waldo was really her little boy Willy who had somehow faked a disappearance, grown a foot and, according to the critics, acquired a way with words. They would travel throughout the country giving lectures and demonstrations. The high point of the evening would come when Waldo and Mrs. Czap would seat themselves before thousands of people and repeat the famous Dying-Mother-Tells-All-About Dead-Son interview. This time Waldo would be madly scribbling away on a notepad while Mrs. Czap moved her lips in time with the tape recorder spinning out the story of Willy's death.

Jasper was disappointed at not being able to play the part of the roving reporter. But his prison record —the unfortunate incident with those little girls and that major swindle—was well-known. Certainly better happiest days of her life, rivaled only by the days she had spent traveling with the theater troupe. But the theater days had been so pansified and soiled by the leading men that she really couldn't compare them. She now took simple pleasure in staying in the background. In newspaper articles on Waldo she was sometimes referred to as Waldo's "constant companion." But that's as far as it went. No one ever made any unkind references to her. People understood completely the quirks that writers have and how sensitive they are about their personal lives. The public could see that Waldo had a talent to reckon with, so they left Clovis alone for the most part.

Waldo took it all in stride. Clovis had been (and still was) kind to him. She was a generous and thoughtful person and one fine day she would die. On that day Waldo would begin her story, just as John had begun the Gladys story, Morris the grandmother story, Mrs. Czap the Willy story, just as his mother would spill the beans about his skin disease and dead hair; indeed, just as all the bereaved flung themselves at typewriters as soon as the last scoopful of dirt was chucked at the foot of the gravestone. You couldn't blame them for it.

It was strange how people now took on a whole new aspect. They *were* important after all. And not just the Johns and Morrises and Mrs. Czaps. No, each single person had a story and those stories were worth money. Everyone—even the lowest on earth—had resale value. The ones like Clovis were worth the most money. They had been places, their stories were colorful and outrageous. Of course if they told the stories they would become household words. If someone else told the story they could share the fame. And if they was all nerved up because of the la-dee-dah; who would believe it and so on. It was decided that she should rehearse her heartbreaking story just in case anything went wrong with the tape recorder. Nothing could be left to chance. She did this gladly and with a tight corset on. The corset made her voice change if it was drawn very tight. She really sounded heartbroken; the remorse strained against the corset, she breathed heavily, and had to close her eyes, she writhed and made pathetic noises. When she became bored with telling the story over and over she stopped, looked at Jasper and said, "Mandrake Club—how do you do!"

"When I say piss up a rope, I mean it!" Jasper shouted at a waitress who asked whether he had a reservation. With that he entered and Mrs. Czap and Waldo followed. Clovis held Waldo's hand.

Jasper pointed to the ceiling. "There's your new home," he said.

Waldo looked up and saw a huge glass box suspended from the ceiling by cables. Inside the thing were a table and chair.

"Shall I get in now?" asked Waldo.

"Might as well," said Jasper.

"I'm going to miss you," Clovis said. "Hurry right down as soon as you finish."

The glass writer's-cage was let down slowly. When it reached the floor a waitress dashed over and snapped the door open. Waldo waved goodbye to his friends and got in. Then the cage was raised into the air where it swayed slightly. Waldo sat down at the typewriter and looked out at the club. He hadn't remembered that it was so pleasant. It was lovely with flowers and green ferns everywhere and filled with people having

"Czap-Czap-Czap!"

Waldo looked at them. They wanted to hear the details. They had had enough of introductions. They wanted flesh and blood. Even Clovis was banging her glass on the table and chanting the name of the bereaved woman. The master of ceremonies laughed and said, "I can see you're all as interested as I am to hear this terrific story. And so without further ado let me call upon Mrs. Czap. But before I . . ."

"Czap-Czap-Czap!"

". . . let her come up here I'd like to take a great deal of pleasure in announcing that today Mrs. Czap is fifty years young. Thankyouverymuch. And now"—a roll of drums—"Mrs. Czap!"

"There's something I want to get straight right off," said the voice from the stage. But Mrs. Czap was just seating herself and smiling at the audience. She did look a bit nerved up. The tape recorder continued in spite of her. She glanced around, heard her voice, then began moving her lips out of time with the words. It was like a foreign film that has been badly dubbed.

The people didn't mind at all. As she spoke they oohed and clucked.

Waldo turned up his microphone and tapped on the typewriter. *Fika-fika-fika-fika.*

The applause was deafening. The heads turned toward him and then back to the stage where Mrs. Czap ran on about the turtle, the bowl, the heartbreak of it all.

Waldo saw that the people were engrossed. He tapped again: *fika-fika-fika.* More applause.

It was like a tennis match. First the heads turned toward Mrs. Czap, listened to the story, then they heard the writer writing it down in his special cage and

As a finale she went to the side of the pool and snatched a hapless duck by the neck and held him up to the audience. There were loud cheers as the duck was held aloft. He flapped. More cheers. He struggled to get free. A standing ovation. Mrs. Czap grinning and wringing the neck of the duck. Flowers tossed on the stage and a splatter of petals.

Once again Mrs. Czap bowed and, shaking her hips, waddled heavily off the stage. When she got to the stage door she blew another kiss to the audience and then flung the duck onto the dance floor as if she were throwing a bouquet of wet flowers.

A crowd of people ran onto the stage to capture the duck. They pushed and shoved and finally made a pulsing circle around the duck, each waiting for a chance to make off with a souvenir.

"He's coming to," one woman said.

"He is not!" said a man. "I can tell he's dead."

"He's alive!" said another woman in protest. "He's sleeping." The woman was indignant. She was wearing a paper hat that dangled foolishly from a hairpin and a long strand of hair. There was a mean frown on her face. A man next to her, holding her hand, took this as an opportunity to place his icy glass against her back. The woman bumped forward suggestively. Everyone laughed, then turned back to the duck.

"He's dead," a man said very simply.

Waldo saw Clovis pressing to the edge of the circle. In the center the golden duck lay on its side, its wings stretched out as if in flight. It seemed to Waldo to be rocking slowly, the white of its belly-feathers in contrast to the gold of its topside. The feathers on its wrung neck prickled. It's beak started to open.

"Your ducks need oxygen," a man started to say

nodded quickly and then dashed out of the circle to a table where he grabbed a bottle. He charged back into the center of the circle, fell on his knees and struck down once.

At the very end of the amber swing the bottle and the golden duck met in an explosion, quick and muffled by the soft body. But the floor was hard and the bottle smashed—glass flew in all directions. The circle of people tightened and huddled nearer the pile of glass and the feathery smithereens of the duck. The man got to his feet panting for breath. The neck of the bottle, still whole, was clutched in his hand. The duck had not even quacked. It gave Waldo the willies.

"Ya see him?" the man said to the crowd. "He almost took off!"

"Christ Jesus," another man said removing his steamed-up glasses.

Everyone puffed and shook his head, as if he had just run a race and was trying to get his breath.

"That was the biggest duck I've ever seen in my life!" one woman said leaving the circle.

Clovis smiled and offered the man some money. The man dropped the neck of the bottle and took the money. Clovis went back to her table and said nothing. The look on her face was beatific.

The circle of people stayed close to the duck, the mound of shards and blood.

So far, so good, Waldo thought on the way up to the hotel-room the next evening. The googly-eyed bellhop met Waldo and Clovis at the door and handed Waldo a small package. He grinned, then walked away.

"What's that?" asked Clovis inside the room. She pointed to the package.

about myself. Yes, I've known some interesting people, but my father, for instance, was a druggist. What difference does it make?"

Waldo tried to make his voice calm. "Well, it makes a difference if you're going to write a book about it."

"But I'm not, so it doesn't make any difference. I'm the only one that can tell if I'm telling the truth or lying. But I'd stake my life on the fact that someone in this world was a starlet, sold a cow, joined a circus, was raped by a juggler, fell in love with a young boy, told him so, and like that. And it might as well be me. I'm rich so I can talk like this . . . and no one is the wiser. It all makes a good story, don't you think?"

"Yes," said Waldo. "It does." He grinned at Clovis in the dark. She could not see him. He kept on grinning.

"Now the present?"

Waldo got out of bed and went to the table. He took off the paper and when he crawled into bed again Clovis said, "From now on I'm not going to lie any more. I'm going to tell you the truth. I'm a very foolish old lady and I was a very ordinary little girl. Please don't laugh when I tell you that I do love you—I'd do anything for you, anything. Sometimes I worry that you're going to run off with someone else. I've told you all those lies because you like lies. You're young enough so that when you're my age and you put all your lies together you'll see what the truth is. Now, after you show me that present I'm going to tell you the truth because I'm getting a little old for lying. But don't be disappointed if what I tell you is boring."

Clovis put her arm around Waldo's neck and gave him one of those kisses—the gluey-wet ones. Waldo fidgeted on the bed and took the present, a pistol, and about Clovis as John, Morris, Fred Wolfpits and Mrs. Czap had spilled theirs. As his mother would someday tell all. You couldn't blame them for it. You couldn't blame him for it for that matter. You didn't have to love anyone for it though. It didn't have anything to do with love.

# ABOUT THE AUTHOR

PAUL THEROUX is the internationally acclaimed author of such travel books as THE KINGDOM BY THE SEA, THE OLD PATAGONIAN EXPRESS, and THE GREAT RAILWAY BAZAAR, and over a dozen novels, among them THE MOSQUITO COAST and O-ZONE. WALDO was published when Theroux was only 25 years old. Theroux divides his time between London and Cape Cod.